TALES FROM ANCIENT WORLDS

This edition published 2011 by Evans Publishing Group
2A Portman Mansions, Chiltern Street, London, W1U 6NR

British Library Cataloguing in Publication Data:
A CIP catalogue record for this book is available from the British Library

Printed by Graficas 94 in Barcelona, Spain, September 2010, Job number (CAG1631)

ISBN 9780237543839

TALES FROM ANCIENT WORLDS

SHAHRUKH HUSAIN AND BEE WILLEY

CONTENTS

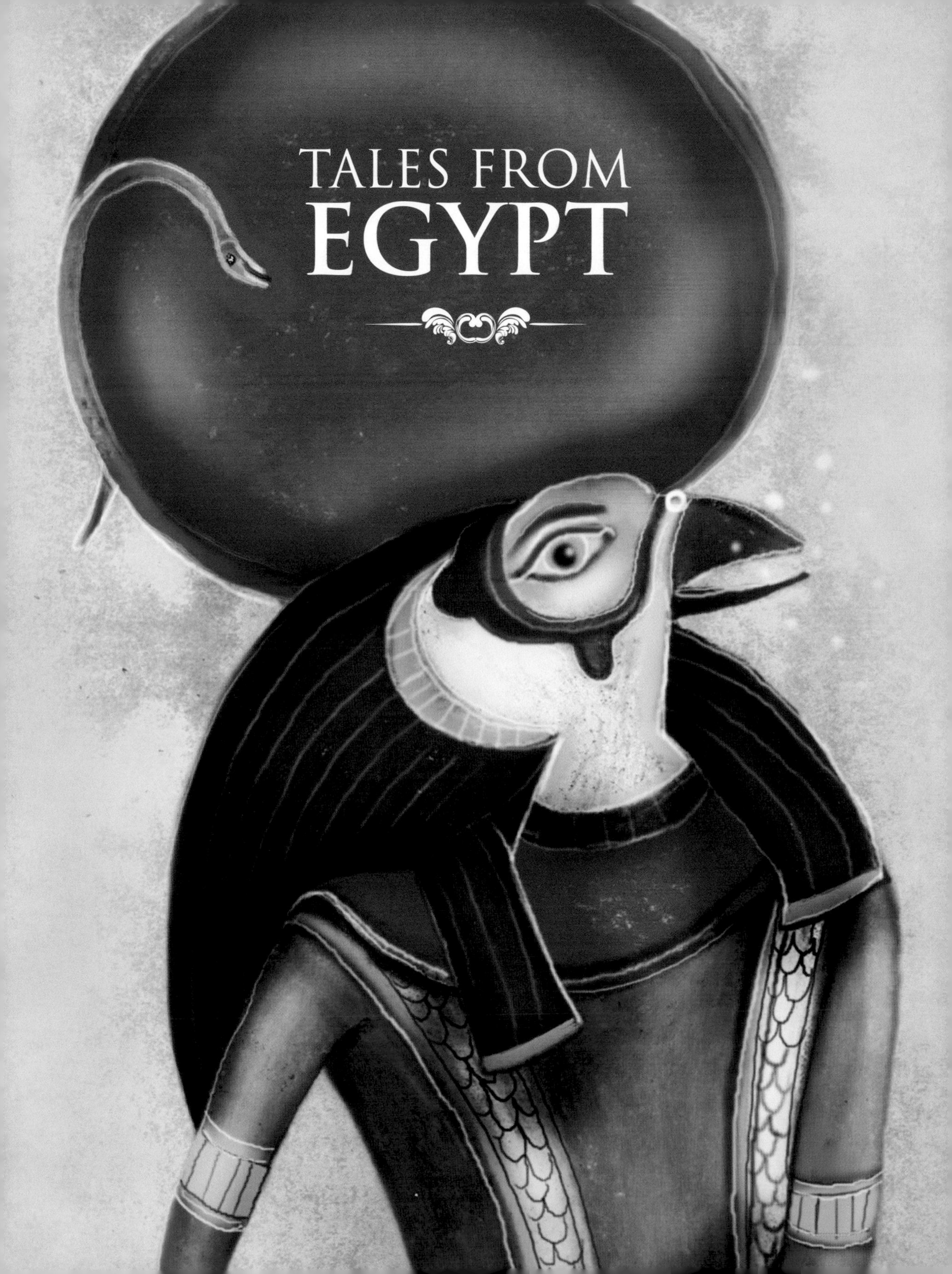
TALES FROM
EGYPT

INTRODUCTION

Egyptian myths existed as far back as 4,300 years ago when they were recorded in hieroglyphs in the pyramids of King Wenis. These myths were meant to help the king safely into the next world and are known as the Pyramid Texts. Other myths were found on scrolls. Fortunately, these scrolls were well preserved so that today we still have a first hand picture of the lives and beliefs of the ancient Egyptians.

Myths are usually about important things like birth, death and the afterlife and tend to have a moral. The story of Isis and Osiris tells us how the Egyptians believed we go to the Underworld after dying. The myth warns that, like the difficult journey of Isis, life holds many struggles but if we try, we can get through them. Egyptian myths are also about the gods and how they brought order and civilisation to the world. This meant that the king or Pharaoh who ruled humans had to be someone with the power to preserve order in the same way as the gods. Myths of the first earthly king, Horus, and of Queen Hatshepsut are examples of this.

The most important god was Atum, the god of the sun. He was present in all of the different creation myths, because without sun there is no life. He is the chief god in the myths of the ancient cities of both Hermopolis and Heliopolis – the two main sources of the Egyptian myths and stories we know today.

The Birth of the Sun God

This is the story of the birth of the sun god and his offspring. Long ago ancient waters, called Neith, covered the earth. Then a mound of earth formed and grew until it stood high above the water. It gave itself a body, which glowed and shone. This was the first being to take shape and it became the sun god and creator god, Atum.

ATUM HUNCHED HIS BODY AND SNEEZED. The rush of air from his mouth became his son Shu, and from the drops came Tefnut, his daughter. Shu was air, dry and crisp. At night he shone out as the soft light of the moon and in the day he became the brightness of the sun's rays. His wife Tefnut was moisture. She was the dew at dawn and the rain of summer that nurtured the crops and she was the spray of the great river Nile that remained in the sands when the floodwaters had gone.

Shu and Tefnut were the first couple and they matched each other perfectly. Now that Atum had two children, he filled the world with gods and goddesses, people and animals.

His work here was done and he decided to go to the heavens, leaving Shu and Tefnut to rule in his place.

Before going Atum reminded Shu to respect the goddess Neith, from whom he had come. She now lived up in the heavens in the shape of a cow. There she held up the stars and other planets who were also gods. Atum, the sun, would join them there to spread his warmth and light. So Shu stretched out his mighty arms, one to the east and one to the west, and he held up the heavens containing Neith. Atum went to live in the sky and every day he travelled the distance between Shu's vast arms, making sure the whole world would be warm and bright.

The Egyptians believed that the sun god was also the creator god. He was called by many different names. In Heliopolis, he was Atum. In Hermopolis, he was Amun and he was also often called Amun Re, or just Re. No one knew his first shape, though some said he had the head of a ram. Mainly he was the sun, bringing life to the world.

How the Year Changed

This story is about the change of the calendar. The sun takes three hundred and sixty-five days to circle the earth and our calendar is based on this cycle, which is why we call it the solar calendar. In ancient times most people timed their months by the cycle of the moon or the lunar cycle.

SHU AND TEFNUT WERE KING AND QUEEN OF EGYPT. They ruled happily with their children Nut and Geb. The family of four lived happily until Atum saw how much Nut loved Geb. Suddenly he was very jealous.

'I am the one you should love most,' he scolded. 'I made you.'

But Nut still idolised Geb.

Atum grew angrier. 'I will make Geb the Earth and Nut the sky,' he bellowed, 'as far from each other as possible.'

But even from this great distance Nut and Geb adored each other. Geb, the earth,

Thoth, the moon god, has the head of an ibis, a bird with a crescent-shaped beak. He wears a loincloth and a long wig.

gazed up at Nut, who formed her body into a great arch and protected him as she gazed down lovingly.

Atum did not like to be ignored. He put a curse on Nut and Geb, saying, 'You cannot have children on any day of any month in the year.'

At last Nut took her eyes off Geb, 'But why, mighty Atum?' she asked, troubled.

'Because,' replied Atum, smugly, 'if you have children you will have even less time for me.'

Nut and Geb were very sad. Nut wept and her tears fell to the ground like soft rain. Thoth, the moon god, who hung in the sky, which was Nut, saw her weeping every night. He felt sorry for her and, being the cleverest god, he came up with an idea to help Nut.

The Egyptians believed that everything existed in pairs – living creatures as well as parts of nature. Night went with day, light with dark, sunshine with rain, and so on. Since the gods were part of nature, they were born in couples, not like human brothers and sisters. So Shu, air, was born with Tefnut, moisture, and together they gave birth to the couple Nut and Geb, the sky and the earth.

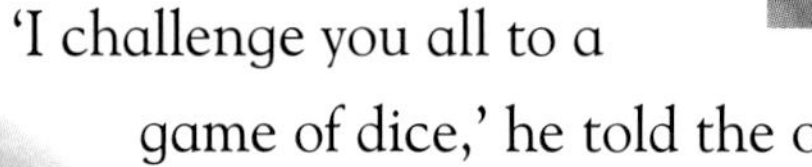

'I challenge you all to a game of dice,' he told the other gods. 'If I win, you must give me what I ask for.'

The gods finally agreed and the game began.

Throw after throw of the dice, skilful Thoth won the highest score. When at last all the gods had played and lost, Thoth sat back contented.

'Do you all agree I have won?' he asked.

'You are the uncontested winner,' they agreed.

'Name your wish,' Atum commanded. 'It will be granted.'

'Supreme Father,' said Thoth, 'I wish for five days to add to the year.'

'Five extra days shall be yours,' replied Atum.

'But what will you do with them, Thoth?' the gods asked. 'There are twelve months, each of thirty days, in the year already. When the moon is a crescent in the sky, we know the new month has begun. When it grows full, it is the middle of the month and as it starts to disappear, we know the end of the month is near. Where will you put your five new days?'

Thoth did not tell anyone about his secret mission. He took the five days, thanked the gods for being good sports and made his way back to Nut.

'You can stop weeping,' he said gently. 'I have a gift for you.'

'Thank you, Thoth,' Nut sighed, without interest.

'I have brought you five days, which I won from the gods in a game of dice,' he prompted.

'But what will I do with five days?' the sky goddess asked flatly.

'Don't you see?' Thoth said, grinning widely. 'These days do not belong to any month. On each of these five days, you are free to give birth.'

Nut raised up her face and began to laugh and her joy and thanks echoed through the universe. Thoth, moon god, god of wisdom, began glowing deeply, and the stars glittered and shone.

Up above, Nut's father, Shu sparkled and shimmered and rained down his light on all of Egypt.

Nut was happier than she had ever been and she gave birth to two couples.

The first pair was Isis and Osiris and the second pair was Seth and Nephthys. Later Isis and Osiris gave birth to Horus, and Seth and Nephthys bore Anubis.

Together, nine of the gods of Hermopolis came to be known as the 'Ennead', which means 'Group of Nine'. They were Neith, Atum, Shu, Tefnut, Geb, Nut, Isis, Osiris and Seth. They later became the best-known gods and goddesses of ancient Egypt.

Gods and Goddesses of Ancient Egypt

Atum (Amun Re),
creator god and sun god

Hathor, cow goddess and daughter of Re

Tefnut, goddess of moisture, twin of Shu

Shu, god of air, twin and husband of Tefnut

Nut, goddess of the sky, twin and wife of Geb

Geb, god of the earth, twin and husband of Nut

Isis, goddess of nature, the moon and healing, twin and wife of Osiris

Osiris, god of agriculture, the sun and the Underworld, twin and husband of Isis

Nephthys, sister and wife of Seth

Seth, god of the desert, darkness and chaos, twin and husband of Nephthys

Horus, god of the sky and earthly king of Egypt

Anubis, god of death and funerals

Isis and Osiris

This story is about the repeating cycles of nature – the four seasons. The death of Osiris explains the winter months when it is cold and there is not much growth because the sun is weak. The disappearance of Isis explains the absence of the moon for ten days each month.

WHEN GEB, THE SKY GOD, DECIDED TO LEAVE HIS KINGDOM, HIS SON OSIRIS TOOK HIS PLACE AS KING. Osiris was kind and wise. He taught the world the secret of growing crops and he brought music and dance to the world. Everyone loved him and his wife Isis, who knew magic and used it to heal people and do good. Only Osiris' brother Seth, was unhappy. He wanted to be king himself.

Seth hatched a nasty plan. He invited Osiris to a banquet and placed a large coffin, called a sarcophagus, in the centre of the room. It was covered in gold, lined with silver and studded with precious stones.

Seth chuckled, 'It is a prize for one of my guests. The person who it fits best may take it home.'

Delighted, the guests climbed in, one by one. Some were too fat, some too thin and most too short.

'Brother Osiris,' Seth smiled, slyly. 'Why don't you try your luck?'

Osiris climbed in and lowered himself into the

bottom of the sarcophagus. Instantly, Seth slammed down the lid and his men secured it with iron bands held together with heavy locks.

'Fling Osiris into the Nile,' he crowed. 'He will drown and I can be king.'

Soon Isis heard the news. 'Seth will not get away with this,' she swore. 'I will find Osiris and bring him back.'

Osiris was the sun and Isis was the moon. With one dead and the other full of grief, the earth grew dark. Because there could be no crops without light, the world became dry and nothing grew anymore. But Isis did not care. She kept on searching for Osiris until one day she arrived at a temple on the banks of the kingdom of Babylon, ruled by King Malchus and Queen Astarte. Isis walked along the riverbank. Suddenly she stopped. She could smell ambrosia, a perfume special to the gods. Her heart leapt. Osiris was nearby. She looked all around her, following the scent until she came to a ditch in the sand where the scent was strong. Isis could see a tree

Osiris is often seen as a mummy, wearing a crown and carrying a crook and a flail to show he is a king. Often he is shown as part of a pillar. His double crown contains the sun disc. Seth is often seen with either the body of a man or a four-legged animal.

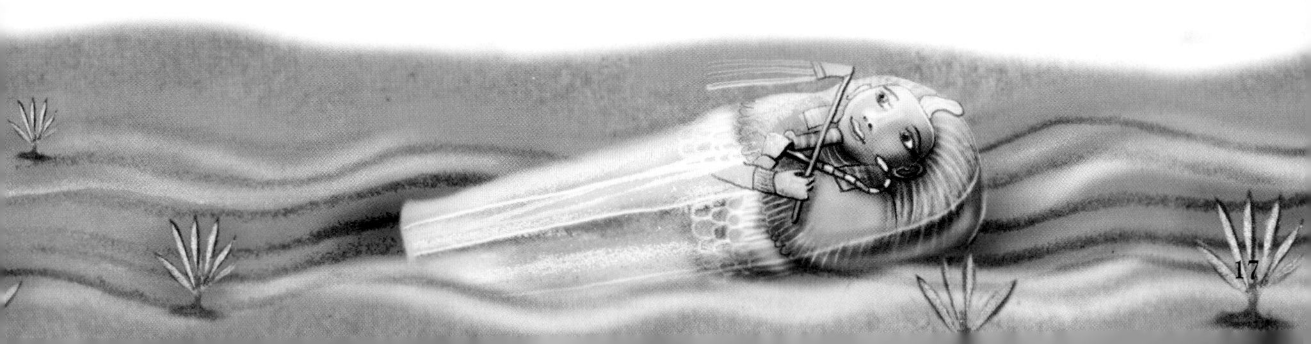

had once grown there.

'Whoever dug up that tree knows where to find Osiris,' she thought excitedly. 'But how will I find out who that is?'

She sat down on the fountain near the temple. Deep in thought, she did not hear Queen Astarte's chariot draw up.

'Who are you, sad lady?' the queen asked, stepping out of the chariot.

'I am a stranger in search of my husband,' Isis replied, 'but I do not know who can help me.'

'Come with me,' said Astarte, 'you can live in the palace and work for me while you look.'

So Isis found herself in Astarte's palace, looking after the little prince of Babylon. One day as she carried the baby into the main hall, Isis smelled ambrosia again. She looked around and her eye fell upon a wooden pillar.

'That is the tree that they dug up,' she thought. The sarcophagus carrying Osiris had been washed on to the shores of Babylon and come to rest against a young tamarisk tree. As the tree grew, its trunk surrounded Osiris and stopped the sarcophagus being washed away, keeping him safe. In return, Osiris filled the tree with his perfume. The king's men, smelling the rare perfume, had cut it down and given it as a gift to the king.

Isis knew she had to cut Osiris out from the tree but King Malchus had looked after Osiris and Queen Astarte had brought her to the palace and she wanted to reward them.

'I will make their son live forever,' she decided. Isis turned herself into a bird and stirred the air until a magic fire blazed around the baby. It would burn away the threads that made people human. That way, he would become immortal and join the gods. The spell took many days to work. Every night Isis waited until the palace was asleep. Then she began her magic. At last, the spell was nearly complete. But, just as it was coming to its end, Astarte walked in and saw the fire blazing with her baby boy in the middle of it.

The Egyptians believed that the sprouting of a seed is like the birth of a baby. Its growth from young plant to ripe crop is like a child growing up. It produces new grain as people bear children. Being harvested is like dying. With replanting the cycle begins all over again. They believed it was the same for humans.

Astarte snatched her child from the flames in fear and panic. 'I was kind to you and you nearly killed my child,' she wept.

'Your child was perfectly safe,' Isis replied. 'I am the goddess Isis. I was trying to repay you by making your son immortal. But you have spoiled my spell.'

Just then the king entered. 'Oh mighty goddess!' he cried, recognising the magic powers of Isis and falling to his knees. 'Please forgive my wife. Tell me how I can win back your mercy.'

Isis took pity on the king. 'You have a tamarisk pillar that I would like very much,' she smiled.

Malchus ordered the pillar to be cut open as Isis commanded. Inside was the sarcophagus of Osiris. She opened the lid impatiently, wanting to speak to Osiris, but he was still and silent. Isis thought he was dead. But then Osiris spoke in a serious and distant voice.

'Re, my grandfather, is the sun and Shu, my father, holds up the skies. Now, as the kings before me, it is my turn to serve the universe,' he said.

'What will you do?' Isis asked.

'I am going to live in Duat, the Underworld. I will be god of eternal life,' replied Osiris. 'It will be my job to make sure that those who have been good will live again after death. You will give birth to our son soon and he will rule Egypt in my place.'

Isis was sad that Osiris was going away but she was happy that he was not dead. She placed the sarcophagus containing his body on a boat and made her way to Egypt.

Isis knew that Osiris would rise each morning in the Underworld and give new life to all the plants that had withered and died while he was lost. The grain would grow again. The flowers would bloom. Once again the sounds of laughter would fill the air. And Isis would recognise the work of Osiris in all those things.

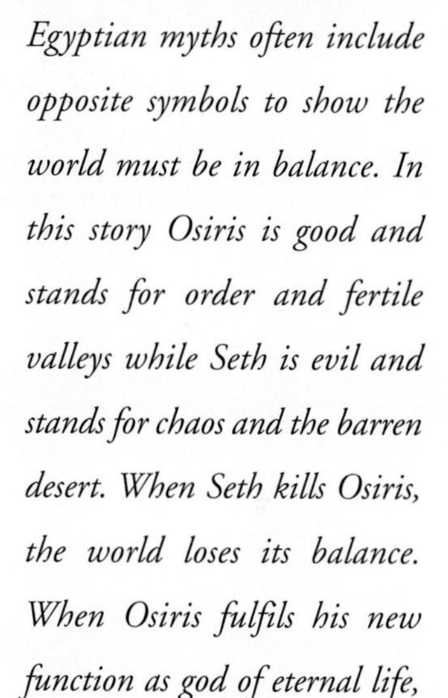

Egyptian myths often include opposite symbols to show the world must be in balance. In this story Osiris is good and stands for order and fertile valleys while Seth is evil and stands for chaos and the barren desert. When Seth kills Osiris, the world loses its balance. When Osiris fulfils his new function as god of eternal life, order is restored.

The First Mummy

This story is about mummification. The Egyptians believed that after people died they moved on to the Underworld to live a new life. That is why it was important to preserve people's bodies and they did this by mummifying them. The words and paintings on the walls of tombs and pyramids were also intended to help people pass into the Underworld.

ISIS BROUGHT BACK THE BODY OF OSIRIS FROM BABYLON and laid the sarcophagus by the mouth of the river in the Delta of Khemmis, the most fertile part of Egypt. She knew that if Seth discovered Osiris' body there, he would destroy it to make sure Osiris did not return to claim his throne. Isis knew it was useless trying to explain that Osiris' work in this world was finished and he had moved to the Underworld to rule Duat, so she hid the sarcophagus in the reeds and rushes by the river.

One day when Isis was out looking for food, Seth arrived in Khemmis with a hunting party. He tramped through the rushes where Osiris was hidden, looking for prey to shoot with his deadly arrows. Instead, he stumbled on the sarcophagus. He recognised it immediately.

'I will get rid of him forever,' he crowed. Seth and his men cut Osiris up into fourteen parts and scattered them throughout Egypt.

Isis was full of grief when she found Osiris gone. Nephthys, Seth's wife, told Isis what had happened and promised that she would help her.

Duat was the Underworld, which Osiris ruled after he left the human world. Plants and creatures go to Duat after dying and are reborn later. Amun, the sun god, journeys through Duat every night leaving the world dark. He later returns to bring day to the world.

They travelled all over Egypt looking for the pieces of Osiris' body. When they finally found them all and put them together, they asked Anubis, the son of Nephthys, for his help. Anubis wrapped the mended body in strips of linen to hold Osiris together to enter the Underworld whole. Soon afterwards, Anubis became known as the protector of the dead and Osiris was the first-known mummy.

Myths of the Eye

The Sacred Eye is an ancient Egyptian symbol of cosmic order and protection and there are many myths written on the subject. This story about the roaming eye of Atum is about how Hathor, a goddess of love and daughter of Atum, came to be part of the later myths of Heliopolis.

For the Egyptians, the left eye was the lunar eye, or the moon eye, and the right one was the solar eye, or the sun eye. Both were shown with two lines below them, representing the tears of Atum, which turned into people. Often, the eyes were decorated with cobras, other snakes or wings. The moon eye was set in a boat with the moon disc, as well as three sun gods, Re, Osiris and Horus, above it.

The Roaming Eye of Atum

Atum, the father of the gods, was sad. He had spent many lonely years in the waters of chaos before turning himself into a god and creating his children, Shu and Tefnut. Now they had wandered away and he was alone again.

'I will create a daughter from my eye,' he decided. 'I will call her Hathor. She will find them for me.'

Hathor looked everywhere for Atum's children. Shu was air and Tefnut was moisture and both were hard to see. So she watched the breezes as they blew and the morning dew fall upon the leaves, until at last she found them and brought them back to their father.

'Oh my children, my children,' Atum rejoiced. 'I'm so glad you have come back to me.' He held them close. Tears of happiness welled up in his eyes and they fell to the earth and became the first people.

Then Atum turned to Hathor, 'As a reward,' he said, smiling his thanks, 'I will turn you into an eye and place you on my forehead for all to see and admire.'

Atum kept his promise and the eye is found all over Egypt in ancient paintings and good luck charms made from silver, copper and brass. Pictures of the eye have been framed and hung in homes for good luck ever since then.

Hathor was the cow goddess and represented joy, beauty, love and marriage. Most other goddesses that were in the form of a cow were connected with Hathor and this meant that they were also considered to be kind and happy goddesses.

In Egypt there was a time when people were wiped out by drought because the Nile didn't flood. People believed that Sekhmet's attack in the story of the Vengeful Eye explains this destruction of the people of Egypt. Pharoah Tutankhamun himself believed that the gods had abandoned Egypt and brought it to ruin, and he tried hard to win back their favour.

The Vengeful Eye of Amun Re

AMUN RE HAD GROWN OLD. He decided to leave the city of Thebes in Hermopolis and become the sun. People began to mock him. Amun Re grew angry.

'How dare they make fun of me? What if I am old?' he ranted.

The gods spoke calming words, 'You are not like ordinary people,' they comforted him. 'Their skins wither and wrinkle but yours glows pure gold. Human bones bend and weaken with age while yours are solid silver. Your beard is the precious and sacred gemstone, lapis lazuli, but age greys the beards of men and makes them drop away. These people speak nonsense.'

'Still,' Re insisted. 'They must learn to respect their creator.'

So Amun Re summoned Hathor. 'Find the people who make fun of me,' he commanded, 'and punish them. And because you are a gentle goddess, I will give you a fierce side. When you find the people who mock me, you will become Sekhmet, the lioness.'

Hathor bowed low and set off on her journey. She found the people who made fun of her father. In a flash she became Sekhmet the lioness and tore apart the offenders. Then, with blood still on her fangs, she attacked again. Amun Re summoned her back.

'I will rest a while,' she said proudly, 'then I will go back and destroy more people. I like the taste of blood.'

Sekhmet's words shocked Amun. 'I wanted the people punished,' he thought, 'not destroyed altogether.'

Amun had to stop Sekhmet. He came up with a plan.

The story of Sekhmet was found in Pharaoh Tutankhamun's tomb when it was discovered in 1922 after remaining untouched for 3,300 years. Tutankhamun was buried with an array of precious gold and jewelled objects, as well as all the things he would have needed for the afterlife, such as clothes, furniture and even chariots.

'Bring the earth from the Red Land of Upper Egypt,' he commanded his gods, 'and mix it with seven thousand jugs of barley wine. Pour them into the fields where Sekhmet will see the wine.'

Sekhmet awoke, stretched and made her way down to earth. Below, she saw fields overflowing with red liquid.

'Blood!' she roared. Immediately she flew down and began to drink greedily. Very soon the wine made her drowsy, and she fell into a deep, deep sleep. When she awoke, the Sekhmet part of Hathor was calm and she returned to heaven, once again her happy, helpful self.

Horus was the sky god and earthly King of Egypt. He was often shown as a falcon soaring high in the sky. He was believed to appear in the skies every July in the form of the constellation Orion, causing the Nile to flood so that the crops would have water and grow. The story of the Shining Eye of Horus tells us the reason why the moon (which was said to be one of Horus' eyes) disappears for around ten days of every month.

The Shining Eye of Horus

HORUS WAS CALLED THE 'FAR-ABOVE ONE' BECAUSE HE WAS THE SKY FALCON. One of his eyes was the sun and the other was the moon. Horus was the son of Isis and Osiris, Lord of the Underworld, and he was set to be king of Egypt. So when he was old enough, he went to his Uncle Seth to claim his throne.

'Never,' said Seth, 'you are just a boy. I will not give you my throne.'

Horus went to the rest of the gods to seek help. His great-grandfather Amun Re, who was still head of the Council of Gods, was on Seth's side. All the other gods believed that Horus should be king.

'Instead of sitting around arguing, let's fight it out,' Seth challenged.
So they fought but neither side won or lost. The struggle raged on. Then, one day, when Horus lay asleep in a field, Seth crept up on him. He gouged the moon eye out of Horus' head and flung it away with all his might.

Immediately the night sky was plunged into darkness.

The gods and goddesses searched hard for the eye but they could not find it anywhere. In the end, they all gave up except Thoth, the moon god, who was determined to return it to Horus. Sadly, when he did finally find the eye, it was broken. Slowly, patiently, he began to piece it together. Then he said a spell to make all the cracks disappear.

'I have brought back your eye,' he told Horus. 'Now you can see again and light will return to the night sky.'

Horus was very happy to have his eye back. And from that day on, the healed moon eye became known as 'Wedjat'.

It is meant to heal people and protect them from harm.

The Birth of Queen Hatshepsut

This is the story of the birth of Pharaoh Hatshepsut, the first female Pharaoh of Egypt. The story is told in pictures on the walls of Hatshepsut's temple to Amun Re at Deir al-Bahri. Hatshepsut was born in 1504 BCE and died in 1482 BCE. She wore the false stone beard of wisdom worn by all Pharaohs. Her story shows how myths and history blended together over the course of time.

Isis is the best known goddess of Egypt. On her crown is the Egyptian hieroglyph for 'throne'. She also sometimes wears a horned crown carrying the moon disc.

AWAY IN THE KINGDOM OF THE GODS AMUN RE WAS DEEP IN THOUGHT. The others sat around him, wondering what was on his mind. At last, Amun spoke.

'Until now all the rulers of Egypt have been men. I think it is time for a change.'

'What kind of a change, Divine Father?' asked Thoth, god of wisdom.

'Isis is powerful and wise,' Amun began, 'in fact, she is the goddess of the throne of Egypt. I see now that there is no reason why a human woman should not become Pharoah.'

The gods gaped at each other in wonder. Was this wise? There had never been a female Pharaoh before. Plenty of queens, but not a single Pharaoh. Since ancient times, the queen was traditionally the person to inherit the throne but it was her husband who always became Pharaoh. It was believed that the spirit of Amun, which was said to be present in all kings, helped them to rule well.

Isis' laughter broke the shocked silence. 'Look at your long faces,' she said. 'What is wrong with having a female Pharaoh? I am willing to guide her myself.'

Isis was a favourite of the gods. She played her sistrum and smiled and joked with them until, finally, they all agreed.

'But,' insisted Thoth to Amun, 'she must have a part of Amun in her just like the male Pharaohs. You must place a female baby in the belly of the wife of the present Pharaoh, Thuthmosis the First, while she sleeps. You will create this baby, who shall be known as your daughter, so that her great qualities will shine out for all to see. In time, she will naturally find her place as Pharaoh.'

The very next day, Amun arrived at the palace and made his way to the chamber of Ahmosis, the wife of the Pharaoh. Standing beside her, he created a tiny bud, which would one day flower into a great woman.

Amun Re was the chief god of Hermopolis. He wears a tall crown with feathers. In Thebes, he joined with Khnum who had a ram's head. In Heliopolis he merged with Re and became Amun Re who had the shape of a human with the head of a hawk. He is also shown as the sun.

The Egyptians believed that there was a part of Amun Re in all Pharaohs and that was why they were respected as gods. Being a woman, Hatshepsut had to prove she deserved the same respect. That is probably why she told this story.

Immediately the room was filled with an exquisite scent. It was a smell more wonderful than flowers or herbs or any scent known to man. It was the perfume of the gods themselves. And, as he placed the bud in Ahmosis, she too, became filled with this glorious scent.

As the baby grew, the whole palace was filled with the wonderful perfume of the gods. When at last she was born, the Pharaoh, her earthly father, named her Hatshepsut, which means, 'part of the best', because he knew she was a gift from the gods.

Much later, as Amun had foretold, Hatshepsut became the first female Pharaoh.

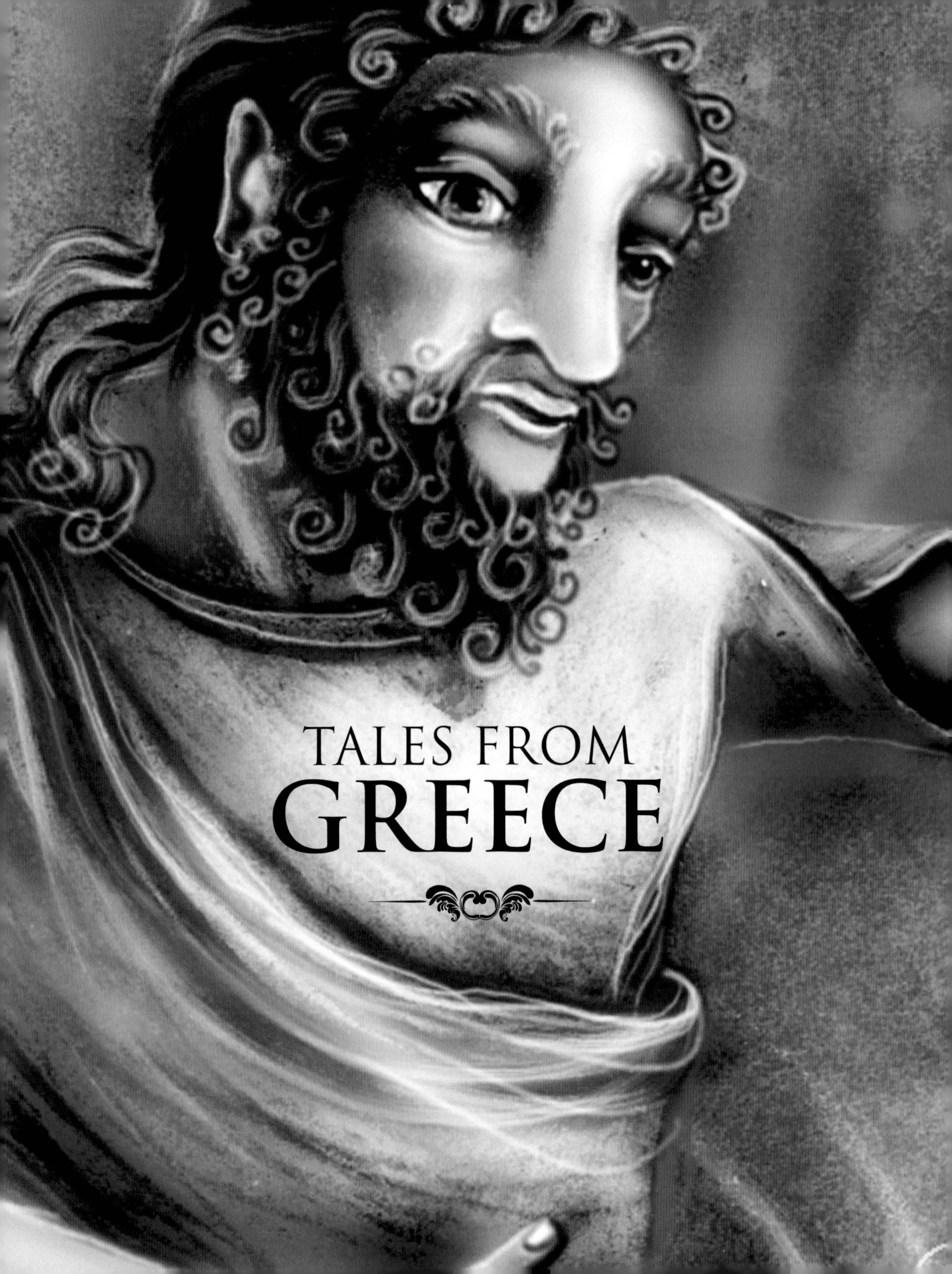

TALES FROM GREECE

INTRODUCTION

Greek-speaking people existed as long ago as 2200-2100 BCE. Their civilisations had disappeared by the time ancestors of the present Greek nations came to power. But from the earliest times, Greek myths have mainly been about gods, kings, heroes and magical animals. The gods are all-powerful and like to use humans to amuse themselves. Heroes are brave men, usually the sons of gods, and they are often up against wicked kings who have seized their thrones and send them on dangerous quests, hoping they will be killed by the monsters they have to combat.

All these myths were eventually written down as hymns and stories. The most famous of them are the epics of Hesiod (circa 700 BCE) and Homer (750-725 BCE) and the plays of Euripedes (455-408 BCE). It is important to remember that the gods in these stories were once as seriously worshipped by people as many people worship their own gods today.

The story of Eurynome tells us how the ancient Greeks believed sinners would be sent to a dark place far underground called Tartarus to be punished. Other myths show that we go to the Underworld after death. The heroic tales, such as the story of Theseus and the Minotaur, show how the most difficult problems can be solved if we refuse to accept failure and use both strength and intelligence to help us.

Eurynome

This story is about the beginning of time and the creation of the world. It reflects the ancient Greek belief that any creature - man, bird or beast - who claimed to be able to match the achievements of the gods was committing a terrible sin, and had to be severely punished for it.

The Greeks believed that a hammer dropped from the Underworld (where the dead lived) would take ten days to reach Tartarus. It was guarded by three one-eyed giants called Cyclopes and covered with roots from Earth and sea. Gods and monsters were sent there to be punished for their sins and were terrified of being imprisoned in its darkness forever.

LONG AGO, WHEN LITTLE EXISTED EXCEPT THE YAWNING ABYSS, EURYNOME ROSE OUT OF DARKNESS AND DISORDER. For a long time she wandered alone, floating on the waves. Then she decided to rest. But she could find no solid space on which to place her feet.

'I will drag earth from out of the sea to make solid ground,' Eurynome decided. She spun around in a wild dance on the waves, whipping up a wind. She held out her arms, trying to catch the wind between her palms, and from her movements, she formed a mighty python.

'I'll call you Ophion,' she announced.

Eurynome danced on until at last it was time to create the universe.

'I will turn myself into a dove,' she said. After brooding on the waves, she laid the universal egg.

'Coil yourself seven times around this egg and keep it warm until it hatches,' she commanded Ophion.

Ophion did as she asked. Finally, the egg split in two. Ophion and Eurynome watched in wonder as the glowing planets spilled out of the egg and took their places in the sky. Eurynome and Ophion settled peacefully on Mount Olympus. They watched the earth hanging in its orbit, slowly filling with rivers and mountains, trees and plants, birds and animals.

Then, one day Ophion boasted, 'How clever I was to create the universe.'

'I created the universe,' Eurynome stormed. 'Not you.'

But Ophion kept arguing. 'All you did was lay

an egg. Any bird can do that.'

Eurynome flew into an immense rage and kicked out at Ophion. The mighty serpent reared up at her. Eurynome lashed out again, knocking Ophion's teeth out of his snarling head.

'Go to Tartarus,' she ordered. 'It is the deepest, darkest place in the universe. You will live there forever with the monsters and other evil creatures.'

Ophion let out a mighty shriek and disappeared, leaving Eurynome alone on Mount Olympus.

'Now I shall create a cluster of seven planets,' she decided, 'and giant gods to guard each one.'

When that was done, Eurynome created the first man and named him Pelasgus.

Mount Olympus is the highest and most famous mountain in Greece. According to Greek mythology, it was where the twelve greatest gods, including Zeus, the chief god, lived (see page 43). These gods became known as the Olympians.

Gaia the Earth

This story is about good and evil actions, and how these can change the world. It shows how it is sometimes necessary for a good person to take action against an evil one – as Cronus did against Uranus – to make sure that the force of good triumphs.

GAIA, THE EARTH, WAS THE SOLID GROUND OF THE UNIVERSE. BUT SHE WAS LONELY.

'I will create a partner as big and strong as myself,' she said. Concentrating hard, she formed Uranus, the sky, who became her constant companion.

Gaia was happy now. Every night, when darkness fell Uranus would come down to her and they would spend many hours together. Gaia soon gave birth to her first children, Oceanus and Tethys. Many others followed. These children were called the Titans.

Suddenly, Gaia had many beings to love and Uranus was jealous.

'I will get rid of them,' he decided. 'Then I can have Gaia all to myself again.'

That night when Uranus visited Gaia, he seized her children and buried them in her body, which was by now covered with mountains and valleys and streams. Soon, Gaia had more children. Five more pairs of Titans followed and there were others besides: the three Cyclopes, who were named after thunder and lightning, and the Hecatoncheires who were giants with a hundred arms each. Each Titan couple gave birth to more children and the universe was blessed with light, stars, sun, moon, planets and many other wonderful things. But every night when Uranus came to visit, he would bury a few more of Gaia's children in her body.

Gaia's body grew heavy and she groaned and twisted with her massive burden. At last, she could bear it no more. She reached into her body, which was the Earth, and pulled out iron to make a sharp, curved blade studded with spikes. Then she called her remaining children together.

'Uranus has committed the first evil deed,' she told them. 'Evil must be punished. Which of you has the courage to punish him and free the rest?'

No one said a word. Then suddenly, Cronus echoed her words.

'Uranus has committed the first evil deed. I am brave enough to punish him and free my brothers and sisters.'

Gaia smiled warmly at him. She held up the weapon she had made.

'This is a scythe,' she explained. 'Hide near me tonight. When Uranus comes, strike him with it.'

That night, Cronus hid in a cave until Uranus was deep in conversation. Then he crept out and struck Uranus hard. With a bellow, Uranus the sky drew away from Gaia the Earth and fled roaring to the distant horizon where he stayed for all eternity. A few drops of his blood fell into the sea to form Aphrodite, goddess of beauty and love.

Together, Gaia and Cronus freed the others and, as a reward for his courage, Gaia made Cronus king of all the gods.

How Zeus came to Power

This story is about the first war and how wars begin. When kings think of themselves instead of their people, as Cronus did, they must be overthrown and this often leads to war. Some people believe that this story is based on a real war that took place a long time before history was written down.

EVERYTHING SEEMED PERFECT IN THE KINGDOM OF CRONUS AND HIS WIFE RHEA. But deep inside, Cronus was troubled. He had once been told that a child of his would take his place as king.

'If all my children die,' he thought to himself, 'I can rule forever.'

So every time Rhea gave birth, he opened his mouth and swallowed the baby whole.

'Stop this,' Rhea pleaded with him. 'You're becoming as evil as your father, Uranus.'

But Cronus refused to listen. So the next time Rhea was going to have a baby, she prayed to Gaia for help.

'Take the child to Lyktos, in Crete,' Gaia told her. 'I'll meet you there.'

Rhea crept away in the dark of night and gave birth to her son in a cave. Gaia took the child and Rhea returned to her husband.

'Where is the new child?' Cronus asked.
Rhea handed him a stone wrapped in a blanket and Cronus swallowed it. Baby Zeus was safe.

Zeus grew faster than any being before him. Soon, he learned about war and wisdom. When Zeus was ready, Gaia persuaded Cronus to meet him.

Zeus bowed deeply before his father. He was charming and respectful and glowed with a golden light.

'May I offer you a small gift?' he asked. 'It is a remarkable herb that was given to me by a goddess.'

Carefully, Cronus examined the food which Zeus was holding out. It looked harmless, so he swallowed it. Immediately, his stomach churned and he began to vomit.

Zeus grew up in the forest, hidden away from his father, and was nursed by a nymph called Amalthea, who took the form of a goat. He was protected by a magical goatskin cloak which, along with the thunderbolt he carried, became a symbol of his godliness.

Out came the stone he had eaten instead of Zeus. Next followed the goddesses Hestia, Demeter and Hera, then the gods, Poseidon and Hades. Led by Zeus, they surrounded their father.

'This is the end for you,' Zeus announced. 'I banish you from heaven. I will rule in your place.'

A thunderous noise interrupted Zeus. The Titans had discovered that their brother Cronus was in trouble. They had not forgotten that he had bravely rescued them from Uranus. In an instant they strode to Mount Olympus, ready to defend him.

The three Hecatoncheires were giants with a hundred arms and fifty heads and the three Cyclopes were master craftsmen, with one eye each in their foreheads. Cronus, their brother, sent them to Tartarus after he was warned that they would eventually help to overthrow his rule.

Zeus and his brothers and sisters fought back. Both groups were strong fighters and the war raged on for ten long years. Finally, Gaia decided to put an end to it.

'Release the Cyclopes and the Hecatoncheires from Tartarus,' Gaia told Zeus. 'Strengthen them with nectar and ambrosia, the food of the gods. Then make them fight the Titans.'

Zeus, Poseidon and Hades entered Tartarus and found the mighty creatures in chains. With a powerful blow, Zeus released them. They promised to fight with Zeus against the Titans and awarded each of the gods special weapons against evil. To Hades, they gave a magic helmet which made him invisible. To Poseidon, they gave an enormous trident - one shake of it could make the Earth and sea shudder and tremble. Zeus was given thunder and lightning bolts.

This time, with the help of the Cyclopes and the Hecatoncheires, the Olympians defeated the Titans. Zeus carried his father Cronus off to the Isle of the Blessed, where he left him to rule forever from the Tower of Cronus.

'From this day on,' said Gaia to Zeus, 'you will be leader of the gods and king of heaven and Earth.'

Zeus remembered his brothers had helped him. He decided to thank them.

'I will give the Underworld to Hades,' he said. 'From there he will make sure that justice is done. And Poseidon will be called the 'Earth-Shaker', master of earthquakes and the oceans and all that is in them.'

Gods and Goddesses of Mount Olympus

Cronus - youngest of the twelve Titans created by Gaia

Aphrodite
goddess of beauty and love

Hestia
goddess of the home and the fireplace

Demeter
goddess of the Earth

Zeus
chief god and god of thunder, lightning and storms

Hera
Zeus' wife and sister, goddess of marriage and women

Poseidon
god of the sea and earthquakes

Hades
god of the Underworld

Persephone
daughter of Zeus and Demeter and queen of the Underworld

Ares
son of Zeus and Hera and god of war

Hephaistos
son of Zeus and Hera and blacksmith of the gods

Artemis
daughter of Zeus, twin sister of Apollo and goddess of the hunt

Apollo
son of Zeus and god of music, poetry and the sun

Hermes
son of Zeus and messenger of the gods

Athena
daughter of Zeus and goddess of war and wisdom

Heroes and Magical Animals

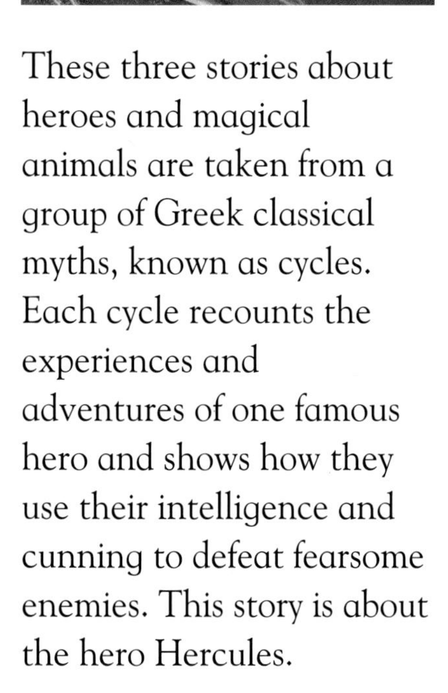

These three stories about heroes and magical animals are taken from a group of Greek classical myths, known as cycles. Each cycle recounts the experiences and adventures of one famous hero and shows how they use their intelligence and cunning to defeat fearsome enemies. This story is about the hero Hercules.

Some say Cerberus had three or four heads, others that he had fifty. A bristling ridge of fur ran down the centre of his back. Snakes grew, wriggling and writhing, from his tail and his shaggy belly.

Hercules and the Hound of Hell

THE GREAT HERO HERCULES STOOD BEFORE HIS COUSIN, KING EURYSTHEUS. The king had set him twelve tasks before he would let him come to live in his homeland of Argos. Many brave men had died trying to fulfil the tasks but Hercules had already completed eleven of them. Now Eurystheus revealed the deadliest task of all.

'Bring me Cerberus, the hound of hell from Hades.'

'But the living aren't allowed to enter the Underworld!' Hercules exclaimed, shocked. 'And no one ever comes back from it. That's why it's called the Land of the Dead.'

'That,' replied the king smugly, 'is your problem to resolve, not mine.'

So Hercules set off across the great river Styx which divided the land of the dead from the world of the living. As the boat drifted to the shore, Hercules caught sight of Cerberus guarding the gates of the Underworld. He was no ordinary dog. His many heads snapped and growled and his eyes flashed blue fire like massive sparks from a flint. As the hound's ferocious barks reached his ears, Hercules thought hard how to conquer him. But as he climbed out of the boat, Cerberus recognised the hero and began to run. Hercules chased after him, until at last they reached the thrones of Hades and Persephone.

'Mighty king and queen,' Hercules greeted them. 'Please allow me to take Cerberus back to Earth to complete the last of my twelve quests.'

'If you can capture him with no weapon,' Hades mocked, 'take him.'

Hercules nodded, knowing this would be almost impossible. Cerberus bit him hard and lashed his tail back and forth. The snakes stung and poisoned Hercules, but he locked the beast in his great arms and held on with all his strength.

At last nearly all the breath was crushed from Cerberus. Hercules slipped a chain round the hound's neck and led him back across the Styx to Argos. The crowds, who had come to witness his triumph, cheered wildly. People could not believe that Hercules had returned alive from the Underworld. At last he was free to live in Argos.

In this very famous story, Theseus tackles the Minotaur of Crete in the labyrinth (maze) where the monster lived. Theseus was a great hero of Greek mythology and had many other exciting adventures.

Theseus and the Minotaur

ALL OF ATHENS WAS IN MOURNING. People crowded aroun King Minos of Crete, crying and beating their breasts in despair.

'What's the matter?' asked Theseus.

'Oh stranger,' replied a woman, sadly. 'Every nine years Minos takes seven young men and women from us t sacrifice to a monster who is half-man, half-bull.'

'The Minotaur!' Theseus exclaimed.

The woman nodded, tears running down her face.

Theseus pushed through the crowds to face Minos.

'Take me,' he demanded.

King Minos looked Theseus up and down.

'You're young and fit,' he chuckled. 'Get on the ship and prepare to die.'

Theseus joined the others on the boat and they set sail for Crete, where they were met by the priestess Ariadne.

'The Minotaur lives in a labyrinth,' she said. 'You will face it alone. If you come back alive, you may go home. But I must warn you that no one ever has before.'

Theseus thrust himself to the front. Ariadne saw his determination and courage.

'You look brave,' she whispered. 'Take this ball of twine. Fasten it to the entrance of the labyrinth and hold on to it. If you escape the Minotaur, follow it back out.'

Theseus thanked Ariadne and entered the dark cave. He walked on until he heard the sound of stamping and snorting. All at once, the monster was rushing at him, bellowing and rearing up. Theseus stepped aside, then attacked it from behind to avoid its deadly horns. A violent struggle followed. At times the Minotaur was winning; at others, Theseus.

The Greeks believed that sacrifices made the gods happy. They offered them sacrifices of grain, wine and honey, as well as animals on special feast days. If they wanted to please a monster, like the Minotaur, they sacrificed humans. They hoped the lives of others would be spared in return.

With the last of his strength, Theseus grasped the Minotaur's horns and wrestled him to the ground, then struck him with his sword. The great beast collapsed, howling. Swiftly Theseus turned, snatched up his twine and followed it out to the mouth of the labyrinth. Then he hid it out of sight so that Ariadne would not be in trouble.

Outside, the crowd stood in disbelieving silence. Theseus really was a hero. The young people of Athens were safe once more.

Bellerophon and the Chimaera

This story shows how heroes, like Bellerophon, may have to rely on quick thinking to succeed in their quests. Greek heroes were often helped by the gods because they defended the forces of good against evil.

The Furies, Muses and Fates were goddess threesomes. The Furies made laws about right and wrong and punished wrong-doers, and the Muses ruled music, learning and poetry. The Fates decided people's destinies.

KING IOBATUS OF LYCIA WAS FURIOUS WITH HIS GUEST, BELLEROPHON. He had been told that Bellerophon had insulted his daughter.

'The Furies would punish me if I killed a guest in my kingdom,' Iobatus thought. So he hatched a clever plan.

'Go to Caria,' he commanded Bellerophon. 'My enemy, the King of Caria, has tamed a creature called the Chimaera. Kill it before he can use it against my people.'

Wisely, Bellerophon decided to ask the advice of a man who could see into the future.

'You must tame Pegasus, the winged horse,' the man told him. 'Sleep in the temple of Apollo tonight. If you are lucky, the gods will help you.'

That night, Bellerophon dreamt of the goddess Athena. 'No man can tame Pegasus,' she said. 'But show him this bridle and he will let you ride him.'

Bellerophon awoke holding a golden bridle and set off, searching everywhere. Eventually, he arrived in Corinth. Tired and thirsty, he stopped at a well. There, at last before him, stood a fabulous, winged horse.

Pegasus saw Bellerophon

and spread his wings, ready to fly away. Swiftly, Bellerophon held out Athena's bridle. Pegasus flicked his mane and came over, bowing his head for the bridle. Bellorophon leapt on to his back and together they flew to Caria.

The Greeks believed that gods spoke to them through people called oracles, who were usually priestesses. People went to oracles to ask for advice about the future. The answer came through dreams or the voice of a god. The temple where the priest or priestess was consulted was also known as an oracle.

The smoke from the Chimaera's fiery breath rose high above Caria. She was a hideous monster. Her lion head roared above the body of a goat and the hindquarters of a snake and she spat flames and poison. Bellerophon shot a stream of arrows at her, but they bounced off her thick hide like twigs. Then he had an idea. He loosened a piece of lead from the binding on his quiver and attached it to the point of his arrow. Carefully, he aimed into the mouth of the monster. The Chimaera caught the arrow and threw back her head to mock him. The next instant, the arrow was ablaze. The Chimaera shrieked in pain. The lead had melted and was pouring down her throat, choking and burning. Within moments, she lay dead.

Bellerophon stroked Pegasus' silky mane.

'Thank you, my friend,' he said.

Then he and Pegasus flew back to Lycia, victorious.

Athena and Poseidon

This story describes how Athena, goddess of war, came to be the most important goddess of the people of Attica. After choosing Athena to be their patron, they won many wars and Attica eventually became an empire in its own right.

LONG AGO, POSEIDON, GOD OF THE SEA AND ATHENA, GODDESS OF WAR, GOT INTO AN ARGUMENT. Each god claimed to be the patron deity of the kingdom of Attica.Their argument raged on for days.

At last, Athena who was also goddess of wisdom, said 'This is foolish. Let us decide by contest.'

So they went to King Cecrops who ruled Attica.

'We will each perform an act to benefit your kingdom,' they said. 'You will decide which is the greater The winner will become your protector and patron god.'

Cecrops agreed and the contest began. Poseidon went first. He lifted his trident and brought it down on a rock with a resounding blow. Instantly, a jet of bubbling water gushed out, forming a large pool. Poseidon stood back, satisfied with his handiwork.

'Beat that,' he told Athena. 'A pond from a rock.'

Athena bent and planted a seed into the rock.

'This is my gift to Attica.' She touched the spot with her sceptre and a tree sprang up, its branches loaded with olives. 'Now, Cecrops, decide which gift is more special.'

Cecrops bowed his head. 'Causing water to flow from a rock shows great power,' he murmured. 'But the sea is visible all around dry land. This tree, on the other hand, is unique. Its fruit can be eaten and used to make oil for food and medicine. Athena's gift will be more useful.'

With a roar, Poseidon disappeared and Athena became the patron of Attica. A shrine was erected to honour her. And in time Attica became known as Athens after the goddess.

Athena sprang out of Zeus' head, clothed in a short cloak and golden armour. She carries a spear and a shield bearing the head of a fierce creature called the Gorgon Medusa, who had snakes for hair. Anyone who looked at the Medusa turned to stone. Poseidon is usually shown with a beard. He holds a three-pronged spear called a trident and the symbol of a fish links him to the sea.

The Judgement of Paris

This story tells how the Trojan War was started. It was a long and terrible war between the Greeks and the Trojans, and many great heroes fought and died in it. It is described in the famous Greek epic by Homer called The Odyssey.

Eris, goddess of strife, was angry. Thetis, the daughter of Oceanus, was marrying King Peleas and all the gods of Mount Olympus were celebrating – except Eris. She had not been asked because she spread bad luck wherever she went.

'I'll teach them a lesson for insulting me,' she thought, throwing a golden apple among the guests. There was a hush when the apple landed. Then someone picked it up and read the message inscribed on it: 'For the most beautiful goddess.'

Three goddesses stepped forward, each holding out her hand. They were Hera, Aphrodite and Athena. Thetis and Peleas froze and their guests fell silent.

Eris laughed to herself.

'Whoever is chosen, the other two will be furious!'

The guests all turned to Zeus, the chief god, but he was too clever to get involved in the dispute. Hera and Athena were always quarrelling. And how would he explain to Aphrodite why he hadn't chosen her?

'Go to Mount Ida,' he ordered Hermes, the messenger god. 'Find a shepherd called Paris. He can decide.'

In a few moments, Hermes returned with Paris.

'Now, mortal,' Zeus commanded. 'You must decide who is the most beautiful goddess.'

The Greeks believed that the gods and goddesses had feelings like human beings. That is why Eris was jealous and the goddesses competed with each other just as humans might.

Paris could hardly believe his ears. 'I'm just a shepherd boy. Please don't make me do this,' he pleaded. But the contest had begun.

'Choose me, Paris,' said Hera. 'I will make you ruler of all Asia.'

'Choose me,' said Athena, 'and you will be the wisest man on Earth.'

'Choose me,' said Aphrodite, 'and win the love of beautiful Helen of Troy.'

Without another thought, Paris made his judgement. 'All the goddesses are beautiful,' he said, bowing low. 'But I choose Aphrodite.'

High up in her dwelling, Eris chuckled wickedly to herself. She had laid the foundation for the biggest war the world had ever seen. Helen was married to the king of Troy, and when she ran away with Paris her husband came after them, starting a bitter war with Greece that would last many, many years.

Apollo

This story is about the sun god Apollo, who was the son of Zeus. It shows us how Apollo came to be linked to the oracle at Delphi and emphasises the importance the Greeks placed on respecting holy places.

LETO, MOTHER OF APOLLO, WAS BEING CHASED BY TERRIFYING MONSTERS. She hid in a grove to give birth to Apollo and his twin sister Artemis. But soon she was on the run again. When Apollo was only four days old, he decided to get rid of the monsters for good.

'Make me a bow and plenty of arrows,' Apollo said to Hephaistos, the blacksmith of the gods.

Then Apollo set off on his journey to Mount Parnassus to find one of his mother's tormentors, a huge serpent called Python.

There, hiding in a cave beside a spring, he found the evil creature. He let fly a volley of arrows on the monster. Badly wounded, Python slithered away under the cover of the grass to the oracle in Delphi. He would be safe in the holy space of the oracle who had been given special powers by the gods.

Apollo knew that Python would not change his ways. He would get the oracle to heal him, then he would find Leto and hound her again. So Apollo fired more arrows at Python and this time he killed him.

'You have been violent in a sacred place!' thundered Zeus. 'Enter the temple now and cleanse yourself.'

Apollo was the sun god and is linked with healing, because the light and warmth that come from the sun ensure good health and growth. Because the sun can see everything from its place in the sky, Apollo is also linked with learning, especially music. His twin sister Artemis was the goddess of women and the hunt. Her shrine is at Ephesus.

Apollo knew his father was right but he was too frightened to face the oracle. Instead, he escaped across the sea to the kingdom of Crete. There he made his way to the king who said prayers to purify him.

Leto heard Apollo was in Crete and took Artemis to meet him there. As they walked together, they saw a beautiful grove and Leto stopped to pray. While she prayed, Apollo and Artemis explored their surroundings. Suddenly, they heard Leto screaming in terror and ran towards the grove. A giant was holding Leto high up in the air.

Together, the twins fastened their arrows to their bows and fired. The arrows pierced the giant and he fell to the ground.

'Anyone who tries to hurt my mother again,' declared Apollo, 'will be seeking his own death.'

Then Apollo returned to Delphi and built a temple there to make amends for his violence in the chamber of the oracle. From then on, the oracle at Delphi became Apollo's most famous temple.

The Kidnap of Persephone

This story is about the seasons of the year. When Persephone returned to Earth, things began to grow again, which meant it was spring. Her eight-month stay lasted until the end of the summer. The four months of the year she spent in the Underworld were autumn, when plants wither and die, and winter, when there is very little growth.

In pictures, Demeter carries a sheaf of wheat or corn, a poppy, a sceptre or a flaring torch to show that she is the goddess of the Earth. She is also sometimes accompanied by snakes.

PERSEPHONE WAS PICKING FLOWERS. 'Mother will love these,' she smiled, enjoying their velvety touch and their jewel-like colours.

Suddenly, there was the thunder of hooves, and a rush of wind. The ground opened up beside Persephone. An arm shot out and snatched her.

'Mother!' Persephone screamed, as Hades, king of the Underworld, forced her into his carriage. Her mother, Demeter, ran to help her but the ground had closed up and there was no sign of Persephone.

Demeter disguised herself as an old woman and walked the world, looking for her daughter.

'Have you seen Persephone?' she asked Hesperus each night, as he let loose the stars into the sky. But he just shook his head sadly.

Every morning as Aurora brought the dawn, she asked 'Aurora, have you seen my daughter?' And Aurora looked at Demeter with pity and replied that she had not.

Demeter soon feared the worst. 'Night and day see everything on Earth and in heaven. If they can't see Persephone, she must be in the Underworld.'

Now, Demeter was the goddess of Earth and all that grows on it. So while she was sad, the world grew dark. Plants began to wither and die. Demeter sat on a large rock. For nine days and nights she sat still as if frozen with grief. On the tenth day, she heard a girl's voice:

'Why are you so sad?'

Demeter looked up. Standing before her was a little girl, holding her father's hand.

'I am Celeus,' the man said. 'Come to stay with us.'

Demeter accepted, explaining she would leave soon to find her daughter.

'I understand,' Celeus replied, sadly. 'My son Triptolemus is very ill. He may die soon.'

Later that night, Demeter secretly arose and fed Triptolemus a mixture of poppy juice and milk. Then she placed him gently on the warm ashes in the fireplace. As she did this, his mother came in. With a gasp, she snatched Triptolemus up.

'Why are you trying to hurt my son?' she cried. Then she saw Demeter shining in the full glory of a goddess.

'I was making Triptolemus immortal to thank you for your kindness,' said Demeter. 'You interrupted my spell, but I will reward you anyway. Your son will be healthy.' The bewildered mother watched Demeter draw a thick cloud around her and disappear.

Meanwhile, the gods were worried. 'Nothing grows in the wild or in the fields. The sun is so strong it singes everything. The rain vanishes altogether or falls so heavily that it drowns what is left. And all because Hades stole Persephone.'

Zeus spoke to Hades. 'If Demeter can't be with Persephone, Earth will be destroyed.'

'Persephone is my queen now,' Hades said cunningly. 'But I will obey you.'

Hades knew very well that Persephone could not return to Earth. The Fates had ruled that no one could leave the Underworld if they had eaten anything there. So Hades made sure Persephone had eaten a mouthful of pomegranate.

Zeus knew the Fates could not be ignored. Yet if Demeter and Persephone were not reunited, the Earth would surely die. An idea struck him.

'Persephone will stay in the Underworld for four months of each year. The rest, she will be with her mother,' he decreed.

Demeter was overjoyed to have Persephone back and all the while Persephone was with her, Earth was fertile and fruitful.

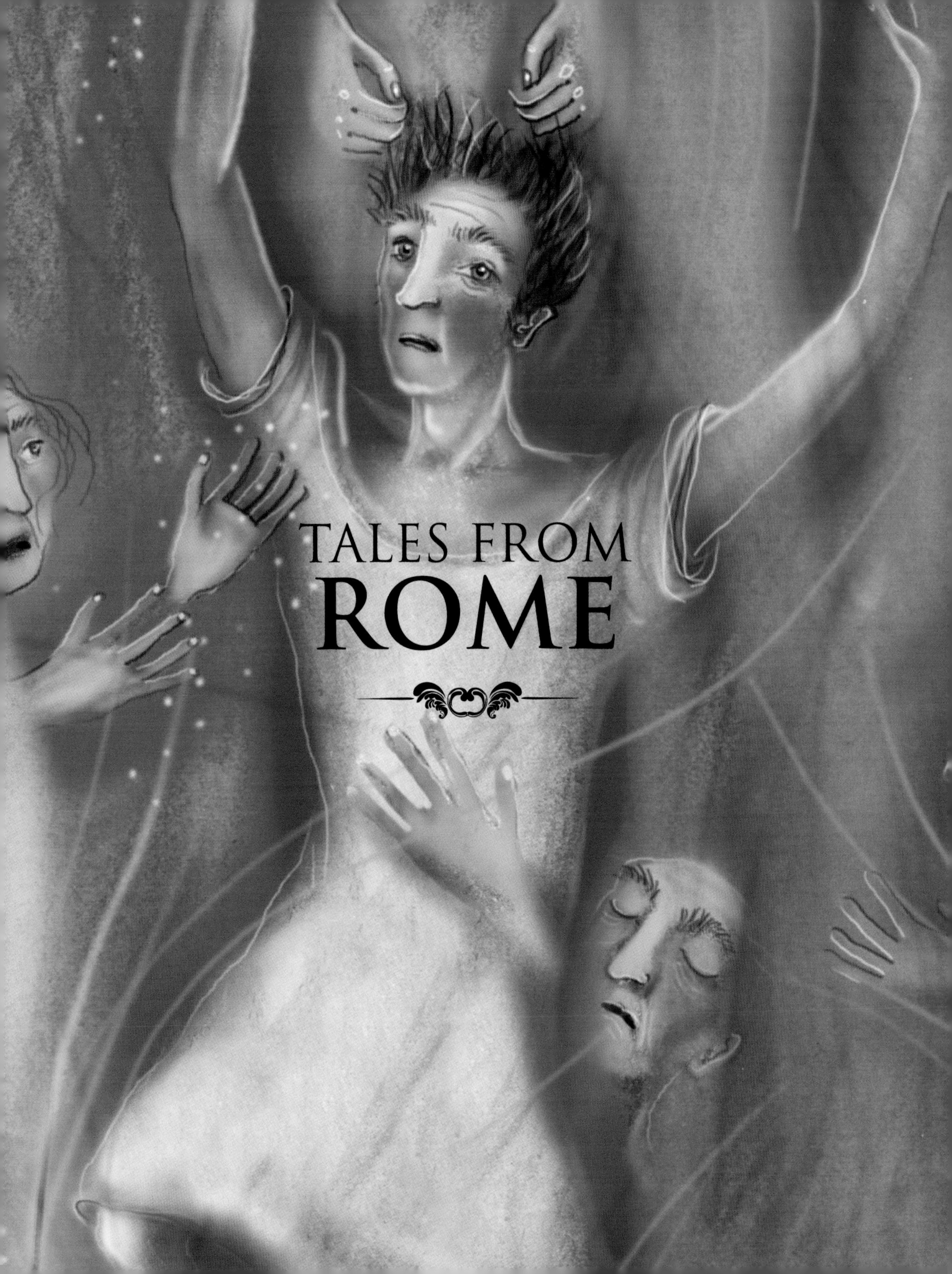
TALES FROM
ROME

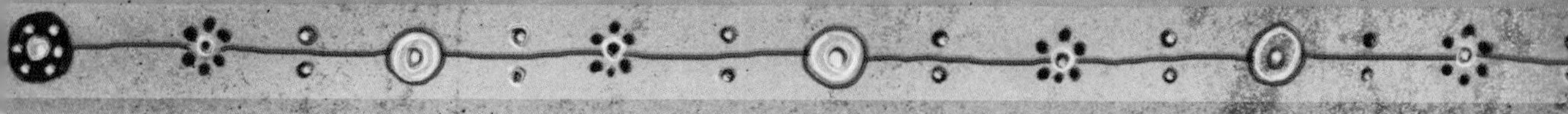

INTRODUCTION

Most Roman myths come from the work of the Roman historian Livy (59 BCE-17 CE), who wrote them as if they were real stories from history. For a long time they were taken to be true accounts and showed the Roman kings as they wanted to be seen – as sons of gods with the divine right to rule. Each Roman clan had its own special family god or goddess known as a tutelary deity. Roman rulers liked to claim descent from the gods. The great emperor Julius Caesar erected temples and statues to Venus and Mars during his rule, claiming they were his ancestors.

The story of Aeneas's visit to the Underworld tells us the ancient Romans believed people go to the Underworld after dying, where those who have lived honestly will go to the Elysian Fields and be happy. The same myth also tells us the importance of rituals in ancient Rome, for we learn that the souls of those who died without proper burial wandered endlessly in search of peace. The Romans strongly believed that the gods helped and guided their actions.

The Romans were a war-like nation, fighting against neighbouring tribes and eventually going on to conquer and rule an enormous part of the world. This is reflected in their myths, which feature soldier heroes, brave deeds achieved for the good of the country, the building of cities and the conquest of lands. The Roman invaders took their gods and myths with them on their travels. As they settled somewhere new an exchange took place. They introduced the Roman gods to the local people and in turn began to worship some of theirs. Old stories blended with new ones and sometimes the same gods were called different names by different cultures. This is particularly true of the Roman and Greek gods, where the Roman gods like Jupiter, Venus and Mars were known as Zeus, Aphrodite and Ares in Greek mythology.

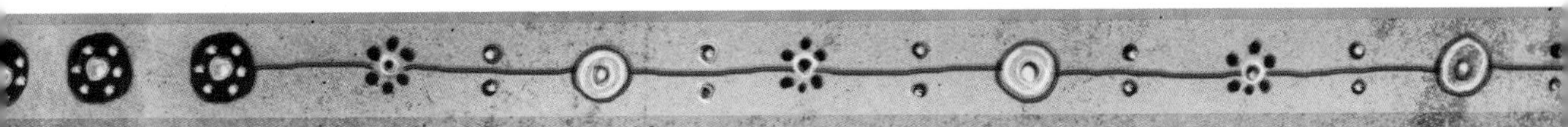

The Voyages of Aeneas

This story is taken from the Aeneid, an epic tale written by Virgil, one of ancient Rome's greatest writers. It tells of the voyages of Aeneas, a Trojan prince, after the fall of Troy and describes the first settlement of Rome. The Aeneid also claims Aeneas was the son of the goddess Venus, which made him a born leader and a worthy forefather of Rome.

TROY WAS BURNING. Aeneas knew he had to leave. He had fought courageously to save it, now it was time to find a new home. His father Anchises was too weak to walk, so Aeneas hoisted him on to his back and set off for the outskirts of the city where other Trojan refugees were waiting.

'Lead the way,' they said. 'We will follow.' They set sail from the port, and soon landed in Thrace.

'Let us rest here. I will light a fire to make an offering to the gods,' said Aeneas. He snapped off a branch from a nearby bush. Instantly, a large drop of blood appeared where the branch had broken.

'Aeneas, brother, spare me,' a voice said. 'I am a prince of Troy. I was sent to Thrace to be protected by the king. Instead, he killed me for my wealth and buried me here under this bush.'

Aeneas was horrified. 'The king's treachery has made the soil of Thrace unclean,' he said to his followers. 'We cannot stay here.'

They journeyed on. In Crete the Trojans planted crops. But the crops failed and the Trojans became sick. So Aeneas and his men sailed on until they came to an island which appeared deserted except for herds of cows.

'At last,' Aeneas rejoiced, 'we've found our new home.'

The men slaughtered some cows and prepared a great feast.

'Let us give thanks for our fortune,' Aeneas began. But a swarm of monstrous creatures swooped down and snatched the food from their hands. Furious, the hungry men struck out at the huge birds, who had faces like pale, hungry women.

'We are the Harpies,' shrieked their leader. 'We will make your lives miserable because you have killed our animals and attacked us.'

The Romans believed that each god had a function. Faunus and Fauna took care of nature and Cybele, Mother Earth, looked after the safety of the land. Venus and Mars helped mainly during war and times of trouble. The Romans believed that their offerings won the blessings of the gods. They created many feasts and festivals to honour them and often visited their temples to ask for advice on important matters. The Romans also asked for their gods' blessings before war and gave thanks to them afterwards.

Aeneas and his men decided to sail on to look for the nearby land of Hesperia. As they voyaged towards it, the sky darkened and the winds rose, whipping the water into huge waves. Some boats crashed against the rocks, casting men out into the sea and Aeneas fell to his knees in despair, begging the gods for mercy.

Neptune, god of the sea, took pity on the Trojans.

'Cease your destruction!' he commanded the winds. Then he told the creatures of the sea to repair the Trojan boats and set them safely on their course.

At last, exhausted, the Trojans arrived in Hesperia.

'Come, Father,' Aeneas said to Anchises, 'let us step together on to the land where the gods have sent us.'

Anchises did not reply.

'Father?' Aeneas said again. But Anchises had died during the storm. Heartbroken, Aeneas told his men he had to find a Sibyl – a prophetess with the power to reunite him with his father. People told him that the Sibyl of Cumae was very wise and powerful. Aeneas searched everywhere until, eventually, he found her cave.

'Take me to the world of the dead,' he pleaded. 'I must say goodbye to my father.'

'It is dangerous but I will take you,' the Sibyl replied. 'First, seek out the golden bough, which grows on a tree in the sacred wood. If you are meant to go to the Underworld, it will come away easily when you grasp it.'

Aeneas stood in the woods, looking around him. Where should he begin? Above him a pair of doves began cooing. Aeneas's spirits lifted. Doves were the favourite birds of the goddess Venus, his mother. The doves flew ahead and he followed until they landed on a small tree. Aeneas looked among its leaves carefully. There he saw, glowing in the darkness, exactly what he was looking for.

'Help me, mother,' he breathed, closing his eyes as he grasped the golden bough. Immediately, it came away and was replaced by another.

He hurried back to the Sibyl.

'Think carefully, Aeneas,' she warned him. 'It is very hard to enter the world of the dead, and to return to Earth is almost impossible.'

'I must see my father this last time,' Aeneas insisted.

The Sibyl told Aeneas to make an offering to Proserpina, Queen of the Dead, over a sacrificial fire which sizzled and leapt. A mighty roar broke the silence in the Sibyl's smoky cave and was followed by the furious barking of dogs.

'The gods have heard us!' exclaimed the Sibyl. 'It is time. Be brave.'

Aeneas felt himself plunging below ground. Flimsy creatures beat against his face. They were the evil beings that made living hard: Hate, Anger, Sickness and Toil. Down, down Aeneas went with the Sibyl, until they stopped on the shores of a black river beside a boat. People thronged around it, but Charon, the ferryman, turned many of them away.

'Why is he turning them away?' Aeneas asked.

'They did not receive proper burials,' the Sibyl replied. 'They will wander the Underworld until their time comes.'

The Sibyl approached Charon, holding out the golden bough. 'Aeneas has brought this gift for your queen.'

Charon ushered Aeneas and the Sibyl on to his ferry. After a long, harsh journey, they arrived at a forked road.

'One branch leads to Elysium, the home of the blessed,' the Sibyl said. 'Let's hope we take it.'

They chose a path. Immediately, they were surrounded by lush fields and clear, tinkling streams.

'I'm sure my father is here,' Aeneas said joyfully.

'I've been waiting for you,' Anchises's voice replied. He embraced his son. 'Continue your journey,' he told Aeneas. 'It will end by the mouth of the River Tiber. There you will create a country which will one day become the greatest in the world.'

The Romans believed that the souls of the dead went to the Underworld. According to Virgil, the soul was made of fire, water, earth and air. Humans were less pure than the gods because they contained more earth. In the Underworld, they were purified in fire, water or air before being reborn. Evil people returned to Earth as savage animals. Noble people stayed forever in a beautiful part of the Underworld known as Elysium or the Elysian Fields.

With Anchises's words ringing in his ears, Aeneas returned to his men and they continued their voyage until at last they arrived at the Tiber. As they landed, Aeneas sent a message to King Latinus, the ruler of the land, to say that they came in peace.

Latinus called his advisors. 'The diviners say my daughter Lavinia will marry a man from foreign lands who will rule my country. I believe Aeneas is that man.'

'Aeneas's fame has spread far and wide,' replied the king's advisors. 'His mother is Venus and Neptune protects him. He is worthy of our princess.'

King Latinus walked down to welcome Aeneas and offer him Lavinia's hand in marriage. At last, Aeneas had led the Trojans to their journey's end.They built a city and named it Lavinium after Aeneas's bride. In time, Rome was built there and the Roman empire flourished and grew, just as Anchises had promised.

The Sibyl of Cumae

This story is about the Roman custom of consulting oracles. The Sibyl of Cumae was one of the most famous oracles or prophetesses. Her name was Herophile and the god Apollo made her life last as many years as the number of grains of sand she could hold in one hand.

KING TARQUINUS THE SECOND LOOKED SCORNFULLY AT THE NINE BUNDLES THE OLD WOMAN HELD OUT. She called them books, but they were really bundles of dried leaves. She said they were prophecies but for all he knew they were just the ramblings of a mad woman.

'The price is outrageous,' he said. 'I am not interested in far-fetched prophecies.'

'If King Tarquinus, the protector of Rome, is not interested I will burn them,' the woman replied.

'Isn't it better to sell them for less than burn them?'

The woman shook her head. 'Better they burn than go to a man who does not value them or Rome's future.'

The old woman was a wise and famous Sibyl who had lived for nine hundred and ninety years in a cave in Cumae. Every time she predicted future events, she wrote them on leaves and left them at the mouth of her cave. Sometimes people collected the precious leaves but others scattered and were lost.

The Sybil carefully placed three of the books on the ground and set them alight.

Tarquinus could not believe his eyes. He had heard about this Sibyl like everyone else. She had predicted that Aeneas would arrive on these shores and build a city. She had even foreseen the building of Rome. Who knew what great secrets of the future were held in those pages?

The Sibylline Prophecies bought by Tarquinus Priscus Lucas, the fifth king of Rome (616-579 BCE) remained in Jupiter's temple until 83 BCE when the temple was burned down. The prophecies that survived were last consulted in 636 CE.

Tarquinus stepped forward, holding up his hand as the Sibyl lifted three more books to fling on the fire. 'Enough!' he commanded. 'You have proved your point. I will buy the remaining books. How much do you want now?'

'The price remains the same,' replied the Sibyl. 'Take it or leave it.'

'I will not give in to you,' Tarquinus said angrily. 'Burn your prophecies.'

'Since you weigh the future in money,' the Sibyl said, 'it is better that I do.'

She swooped to the ground and set three more books alight.

Tarquinus could take no more. 'I will buy the other three for the price of all nine!'

The Sibyl handed the books to Tarquinus. 'Keep them safe and consult them in hard times and in times of confusion. I will not be here much longer but my words will guide you. You have judged well.'

Tarquinus placed the books in the temple of Jupiter where they would be tended by priests and consulted for advice when needed.

The Sibyl returned home. She was expecting a letter. She turned it over and looked at the seal which was made from the earth of Erythrae, her home. The feel and sight of her country's soil after hundreds of years warmed the Sibyl's heart.

'At last,' she thought, 'I can die in peace.'

She had done Rome an immense service. She had left behind her prophecies to guide it to greater and greater glory in the years to come.

Romulus and Remus

This story is about the godly beginnings of Rome's rulers, Romulus and Remus. With Mars as their ancestor, the descendants of Romulus and Remus could claim great power and the right to be king. The story also mentions Vesta, goddess of the home, whose fire burned day and night in the Forum in Rome. The Forum was the centre of religion, business and politics in the city.

The Vestal virgins who served in Vesta's temple inside the Forum were selected from important families and carefully trained for their duties. These were to tend the eternal fires of Vesta and to mix the offerings of grains for public ceremonies.

The Sons of Rea Silva

REA SILVA WAS THE DAUGHTER OF KING NUMITOR OF ALBA LONGA. Her uncle Amulius had snatched the throne from her father and exiled him to the countryside. It made her furious to think that her father, betrayed by his own brother, was wandering helplessly somewhere. She wanted to pay Amulius back by having a son who would win back the kingdom. But Amulius intended to stop her.

'I am going to honour you,' Amulius told her, 'by making you a Vestal virgin. You will dedicate your life to serving at the goddess Vesta's shrine.'

Rea's plan was shattered. The Vestal virgins did not marry for many years, so she would never be able to have sons. Still, she accepted. If she refused, she would be killed and then there would be no one to help her father.

Rea worked hard at the shrine of the goddess and, each day, asked the gods to help her. Then, one morning when she was out in the woods collecting water for the temple, a huge, glowing figure appeared in front of her.

'Do you know who I am?' the figure asked.

'You must be a god,' she replied, falling to her knees.

'I am Mars,' replied the figure. 'Go in peace and continue to serve Vesta. I shall grant your prayers.'

Mars, the god of war, can be recognised by his helmet with a plume and is accompanied by his favourite animals, a wolf and a woodpecker. His festival takes place in March – the month named after him.

Rea told no one about her meeting with Mars but as she went about her daily duties, she often wondered what he could have meant. She knew that the only way she could help her father was by having a son and that just wasn't possible while she served at the temple.

One morning, she found the answer to her question. Two beautiful baby boys lay gurgling beside her when she woke. Mars had sent her two sons who would have the power to restore the throne to her father.

'I must hide them,' Rea thought in a panic. 'The priests will never believe the boys were a gift from Mars. They will kill me or expel me from the temple.'

Just then, the door to her chamber burst open with a bang. Three soldiers marched in.

'Take the children!' commanded the captain. The others lunged forward. Rea clutched her babies, crouching to protect them with her body. One soldier dragged her away while the other grabbed the infants.

'Throw them into the Tiber,' the captain commanded.

'Let me take them far away where we are strangers,' Rea begged.

'I promise they'll never be seen in Alba Longa again.'

The captain and his men took the infants and walked out without another word. Rea fell to her knees, crying out to Mars to save her sons.

'Your Majesty,' the captain reported to Amulius. 'Rea Silva's boys are at this very moment on their way to the Tiber to be fed to the waters.'

Amulius laughed loudly. 'The river is in flood,' he bellowed. 'They will drown at once!'

The Tiber was indeed in flood. Its water whirled and gushed right up to the highest boundary, then ebbed, leaving shimmering pools behind on the river's banks. The soldiers saw the waters swell and burst their banks, then rise, spiralling upwards. Quickly they threw the little boys into the waves and fled. The babies floated on the water as it gushed over a mound of sand at the base of a fig tree. But as the floods retreated, their little bodies were left resting on the mound. Miraculously, the floods had worked in their favour.

At dawn, a she-wolf wandered down to the water's edge looking for something to feed her cubs. Her sharp eyes picked out a movement at the foot of the fig tree. Her keen nose sniffed out the scent of flesh. Slowly, carefully, she edged her way to the twin boys.

Then, just as she reached them, they began to cry. The she-wolf sensed that these infants were hungry for food and comfort, just like her own cubs.

Suddenly, her hunting instincts disappeared. She lay down beside the baby boys, encircled them with her furry body and began suckling them. When they had fallen asleep, she stayed awhile, giving warmth to their tiny bodies. Soon the king's herdsman Faustulus would let loose the royal herds and flocks to graze in the nearby pastures. The she-wolf would find a suitable catch for her cubs then.

In ancient times, there was a hut on the Palatine Hill that people believed to be the home of Faustulus and Larentia. When Faustulus died, he was buried in the Forum in Rome. Later, his tomb was decorated with a lion sculpture to honour him.

Faustulus let his eyes wander as he approached the pastures. He loved this time of morning when all was quiet and the world of men was mostly asleep. His eyes came to rest on the fig tree and he saw the she-wolf curled around the infants. He raced up to the tree as the she-wolf gently detached herself and loped away.

Faustulus fell to his knees and examined the babies. They were warm and healthy. Their small bodies bore no sign of any scratches or bites. Faustulus lifted the babies, looking into their faces.

'Praise the gods,' he cried out. 'That she-wolf has been feeding them. Her milk is still on their lips.'

Leaving the king's animals to graze peacefully, he hurried home to his wife, holding the twin boys close to his chest.

'Larentia,' he called. 'I saw a miracle today!'

Larentia took the babies from her husband and cradled them gently in her arms.

'The gods have sent us two sons,' she whispered. 'Their names will be Romulus and Remus.'

And so Rea Silva's sons were safe.

The Foundation of Rome

This story is found in Books From the Foundation of the City by the famous Roman historian, Livy (59 BCE - 17 CE). It describes how Romulus eventually discovered his true origins and became the rightful founder and first ruler of the city of Rome.

Rome was built across seven hills. The Aventine Hill, overlooking the River Tiber, is in the far south of where Rome is now. The Capitoline Hill, also known as the Aix, is the smallest of the hills, and the Palatine, where the kings' palaces were later built, was the most important.

LUPERCALIA, THE SPRING FESTIVAL, WAS COMING SOON. Romulus and Remus were looking forward to it and so were all their friends. Prayers would be offered to please the god and goddess of nature, Faunus and Fauna, so that the fields and valleys around the Palatine Hill would be fertile again this year. There would be fun and games for everyone.

Romulus and Remus were much admired. They were the strongest young men in the region, the fastest runners, the most agile athletes. All the other young men wanted to be like them. Their parents, Faustulus and Larentia, were very proud of them. The boys had brought them good luck. Since their arrival, Faustulus and Larentia's family had been happier, healthier and wealthier.

The young men were preparing for the festival.

Romulus stood at the starting point, ready to run his race while his father watched. Some distance away, Remus showed off his enormous strength. He completed the final test and walked from the ring, amid cheers, to where Larentia stood watching.

Above the cheers, Remus heard a voice calling. 'Remus! Help me, Remus! Bandits have stolen my cattle.'

Immediately, Remus ran to help. He followed the cattle tracks until he came to a remote area. Darkness was falling but Remus knew his way well. The sound of lowing told him the herd was nearby. Remus flexed his muscles and crept silently towards it. The next moment, he was surrounded by bandits.

'This is the end of you,' growled the thugs. 'We are taking you to the owner of these lands to be put to death.'

'Huh!' snorted Remus. 'Why should he kill me for chasing criminals?'

'You and your brother have troubled us for years,' snarled the leader, ordering his men to gag Remus. 'Now we will have our revenge.'

They bound Remus's hands and marched him to the landowner.

'My lord,' said the bandit leader. 'This man and his brother make regular raids on your lands. They deserve to be severely punished.'

'Put him to death,' commanded the landowner. Remus tried to explain that he and his brother raided only the hiding places of the bandits who lurked in the area. But the landowner would not listen.

Back on the Palatine Hill, a messenger brought Romulus the news that Remus had been condemned to death.

'Go to him immediately,' Faustulus ordered.

Romulus was surprised. 'Isn't it better to make a rescue plan?'

Faustulus shook his head. 'The landowner Numitor is your grandfather.' Faustulus then told Romulus the whole story – how Amulius had stolen the throne from his brother Numitor and had Rea Silva's sons thrown to the floods. 'That is when I found you,' he said, 'suckling on a she-wolf. When I discovered who you were, I said nothing in case Amulius tried to kill you. But now it is time to tell the world who you really are.'

Romulus said goodbye to his parents and went straight to Numitor. 'Remus and I are your grandsons,' he told him. 'We will fight King Amulius and win back your throne.'

Numitor could hardly believe his luck. Together with his grandsons, he defeated the evil Amulius and freed their mother, Rea Silva. Numitor's family was together again. As they helped their grandfather rebuild his kingdom, Romulus looked around him and saw that their homeland was becoming crowded.

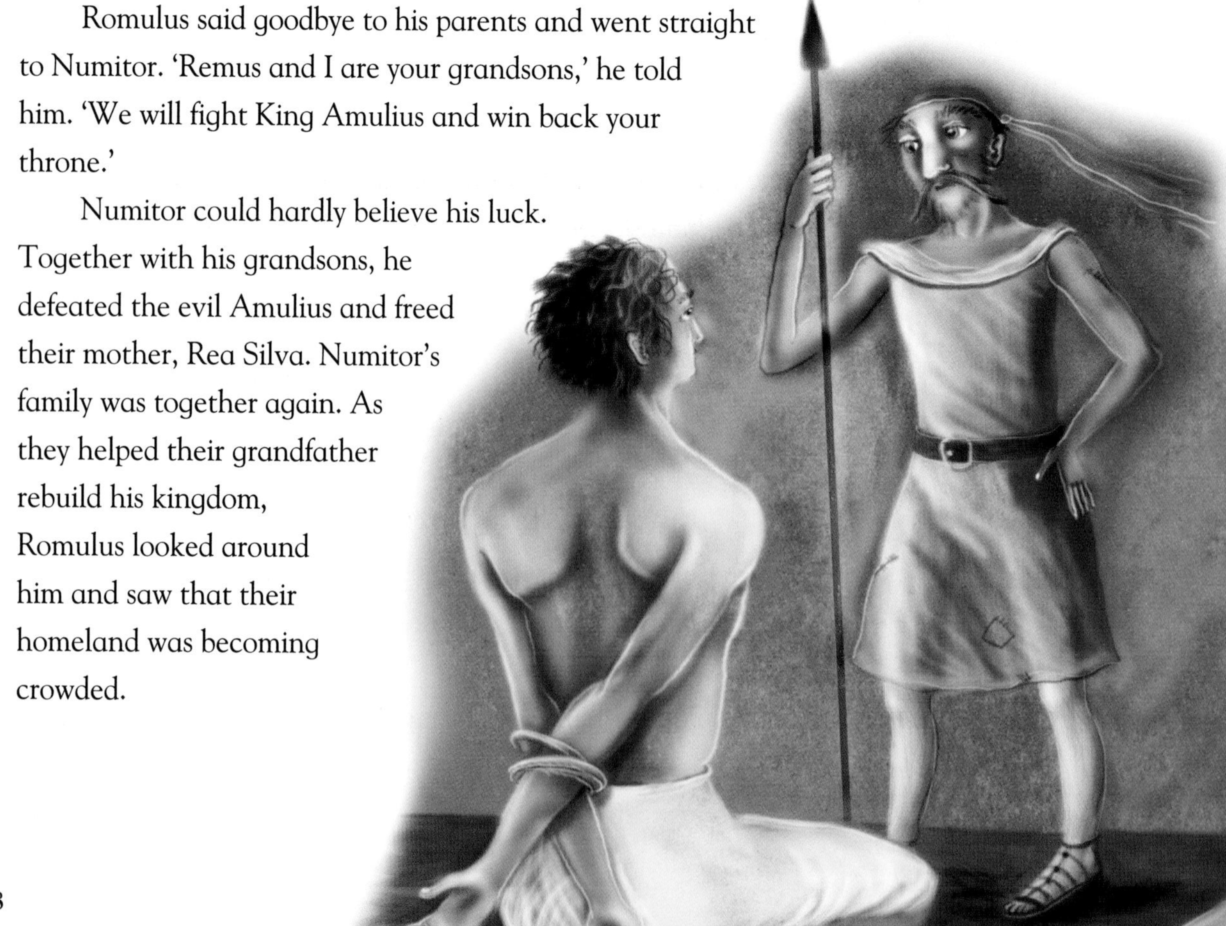

'I shall build a new city,' he declared, 'on the banks of the Tiber where Faustulus found me.'

'I was there, too,' said Remus. 'I should build it.'

The twins turned to Numitor and Rea Silva.

'The older brother has first choice,' said Numitor.

'But they are the same age,' Rea replied.

'Then we must ask the gods to help,' Numitor decided.

So Romulus went to the Palatine Hill and Remus went to the Aventine. Each brother prayed to the god of that place to send him a sign saying who should build the new city and become its ruler.

Remus came back first. 'The gods chose me,' he said. 'Six magnificent vultures appeared to me and took flight. That was surely the sign.'

As people rejoiced, Romulus returned. 'I saw twelve vultures spread their wings and soar into the heavens. The gods want me to rule the new city.'

The Romans believed that Romulus and Remus were the descendants of Aeneas and belonged to a very ancient race. Livy wrote that Romulus built Rome on 21 April 753 BCE. A festival called Parlia marked its foundation. Romulus ruled Rome for thirty-three years. He disappeared mysteriously at the age of fifty-four and it was widely believed that he became the god Quirinus, the protector of warriors and crops.

While people argued who was right, Romulus began his task. 'I will build the boundaries of my city first, to show that it is impregnable,' he said.

When Remus heard his brother's words, he mustered all his strength and leaped over the walls, shouting, 'That's what I think of your city and its boundaries!'

Enraged by Remus's act of mockery, Romulus attacked and killed him. Then he thundered at the gathered crowd, 'And so will perish anyone else who leaps over my walls.'

In the time that followed, Romulus built a strong and powerful city which became one of the most famous in the world. It was named Rome in his honour.

Numa Pompilius

This story is about the way the Roman laws of worship and citizenship were made by Numa Pompilius in 716 BCE. The story also tells us that Numa invented the calendar. When he found that the cycles of the sun were longer but more regular than those of the moon, he added a day to some months to make them even.

ONE YEAR AFTER THE DEATH OF ROMULUS, THE ROMANS CHOSE THEIR NEW KING. He was Numa Pompilius, from the Sabine town of Cures.

'I shall ask the gods for a sign to see if I deserve to be the king of Rome,' Numa told his high priest.

The priest covered Numa's head with a scarf and began the ceremony. He seated Numa on a stone facing south and sat to the right of him. The priest pointed skywards with a crooked rod, knotted in the middle, then drew a circle with it.

The Romans believed that the god Jupiter was the protector of Rome. He was often confused with Zeus, the supreme god of the Greeks, because like Zeus he was god of the sky, rain, thunder and lightning. But the Romans also worshipped Jupiter for his role as the protector of law, fairness and goodness.

With his hand on Numa's head, he said, 'Father Jupiter, this man, Numa Pompilius, wants your permission to be king of Rome. If he has your blessing, show us light. If not, let the sky grow dark.'

The crowd that had gathered to watch the ceremony waited in silence. Suddenly, there was the sound of mighty thunder. Lightning flashed across the heavens. Jupiter had sent his sign. The gathering burst into loud cheers. They had a king!

'Romulus led you to glory,' Numa said. 'Now it is time to make laws of citizenship and proper worship.'

Roman men had fought for so long that they had forgotten how to live in peace, without a spear in their right hand and a shield in their left. Numa told them that the goddess Egeria revealed new laws to him each night as he prayed.

Janus was the oldest Roman god. He was famous for having two faces. Since the time he had helped defend Rome against the Sabine army, the door to his temple had been left open. By closing the door, Numa showed that the Romans did not need Janus's help because there would be no war.

Then Numa walked into the centre of Rome and closed the door of the god Janus's temple. He declared, 'When the door to the temple is closed, we are at peace. When it is open, we are at war.'

Later, Numa decided that the year would be divided into twelve months and that certain days of the year would be set aside for worship and rest. This was the beginning of public holidays as we know them today.

Juno's Warning

This story is about historical events which took place in 384 BCE. The Gauls were Celtic people from northern Italy who attacked and took over much of Italy around Rome. Over the years, archaeologists have uncovered a great deal of evidence of their attack on the city.

ONE DAY A YOUNG ROMAN MAN, PONTIUS COMINUS, SKIMMED ALONG THE RIVER TIBER. He balanced on a strip of cork just large enough to stand on. He was bringing an urgent message to the Senate in Rome, asking for help against the Gauls who were threatening to attack the Capitoline Hill.

The strip of cork floated easily on the water. When the Tiber was calm, he stood on it, using his arms to remain balanced. When the waters were

choppy, making the cork bob and toss, he lay flat on his belly. At moments the waves were so frightening he thought his end had come and he prayed to the gods to let him complete his mission. At last, far in the distance, he spotted the Citadel of Rome standing on the Capitoline Hill.

Pontius crept through the Gaul barricades and scaled a craggy cliff to reach the Senate. The message was well received. The senators agreed to help defend Rome against the Gauls. Pontius retraced his steps through the Gaul barricades, armed with the good news.

The leader of the Gauls discovered Pontius's tracks and was furious.

'Get yourselves ready, men!' he commanded. 'Let's attack the Citadel of Rome and show the Romans who's best.'

As the stars began to light the sky, the Gaul leader nudged the man next to him, and he the man next to him, until all the men were up and armed and ready to go. Very quietly, they moved towards the Capitoline Hill where the Citadel stood, stopping at a cliff so steep that it had been left unguarded. The men secured themselves to the cliff face, each one attaching himself to the arm of the one below, to form a human rope. They worked in complete silence: not the clatter of a rock, nor the squawk or flutter of a bird gave away their movements. Even the sharp-eared dogs of the city heard nothing.

Very soon, the man at the head of the human rope could see the crest of the cliff directly above his head. 'We shall reach the cliff top in less than an hour,' he thought. 'Rome will be in our hands tonight.'

In the Citadel, the night silence was shattered. Marcus Manlius, the Consul of Rome, sat up in bed with a start. What was that terrible noise? He strode to the window, trying to place the sound. It was coming from the geese in the temple of Juno at Arx.

'Why are they clamouring at this time of night?' he wondered. Then it struck him. 'Rome is in danger!'

Instantly, he took up his weapons and called his men to arms. Within moments, they covered the cliffs around the city and found the human rope woven by the bodies of the Gauls. Rushing to the cliff edge, Marcus struck the Gaul leader hard. The man lost his grip and toppled, taking his companions with him.

When morning came, the people of Rome heard what had happened and brought gifts for the soldiers.

'The goddess Juno protected us last night,' Marcus told them. 'We must thank her.'

And to remember that Marcus Manlius had saved Rome, the people of Rome named him Marcus Capitolinus after the Capitoline Hill.

Juno, the wife of Jupiter and chief goddess, wears a goatskin and carries a spear and a shield. She is often seen with a peacock, her favourite bird. With Jupiter and Minerva, goddess of wisdom, Juno formed the Capitoline Triad. A temple was built to honour them in the Capitol, which was a religious and military centre in Rome.

TALES FROM THE VIKINGS

INTRODUCTION

Viking myths are part of the wider tradition of Norse mythology, which includes most of the Scandinavian countries, as well as other parts of Europe, particularly Germany. They are recorded in three collections, the anonymous Poetic Edda (late 13 CE), the Prose Edda, put together by Snorri Sturluson (early 13 CE) and in the verse of court poets known as skalds (900CE- 1400 CE).

Viking myths are mostly about the adventures of the gods and how they fight the chaotic forces of nature, represented by frost giants, dragons and monsters. The myths also often describe encounters between the gods and humans, as for example Odin advises Prince Sigurd how to defeat the monster Fafnir.

Viking warriors were fierce and daring in battle because death in battle was considered to be more honourable than death from sickness or old age. The Vikings believed that when heroes died fighting they went to Valhalla, the hall of heroes, ruled by the father of the gods, Odin. In Valhalla they feasted and revelled until Ragnarok, or the end of the world, when they would help the gods in a mighty clash between good and evil. The Viking Underworld, Hel, where people went after dying of sickness or old age, is described in the story of Baldur.

Like most people in ancient times, the Vikings travelled huge distances, searching for food and shelter. They voyaged over land and sea covering a vast part of the world, from Greenland in North America to Europe and the Middle East. When they conquered new lands, they usually brought their own gods and myths with them. As they settled, an exchange took place. They introduced their gods to the local people and in turn began to worship some of theirs. For example, Viking beliefs about dwarf craftsmen, magical blacksmiths and most particularly, Odin, the father of the gods, can still be found in Britain today.

The Mother of Water

This account of the creation of the world is taken from the Finnish epic, Kalevala. Its fifty poems, which were written by Elias Lonrott in 1835, contain some of the oldest tales of Scandinavia.

BEFORE TIME BEGAN, A TEAL FLEW THROUGH SPACE, LOOKING FOR SOMEWHERE TO BUILD A NEST. She looked north and south, east and west but all she saw around her was churning water.

'If I lay my eggs on the waves, they'll drift away and smash,' she thought. 'If I lay them in the air, they'll be blown away. What shall I do?'

Deep down in the ocean, the Mother of Water heard her plea and raised her mighty knee above the water.

The teal saw the knee, lush with grass, high above the blue water. It was the perfect place for her nest. When it was built, she laid six eggs of gold and a seventh of iron. Then she perched on the eggs and began to brood.

On the first day, the eggs grew warm and the heat filtered through to the knee of the goddess. On the second day, her skin became hot. On the third, it began to scorch. In pain, she jerked her knee back under the sea. The eggs scattered from the nest, rolled into the water and smashed. Then slowly, as the teal and the goddess watched in amazement, they began to transform. The lower half of the eggs rose high above and formed the dome of the skies. The yolks gleamed and became the dazzling sun. The egg whites shimmered silver and formed the globe of the moon. The pieces of shell were transformed into a million stars and the iron scraps turned into dark clouds. And that was how the world was formed.

The Vikings called the sun goddess Sol and the moon god Mani. The two gods rode across the sky on horse-drawn chariots, chased by wolves, exchanging places at dawn and dusk. The Vikings believed that one day the wolves would catch the sun and the moon and swallow them, ending the cycle of night and day and bringing about the end of the world. The Vikings called the end of the world Ragnarok.

Ymir, the Frost Giant

The fight between the frost giants and the gods is another Viking tale of creation. It explains the bitter cold of Scandinavian countries and may even refer to one of the ice ages. The later Vikings travelled as far south as Turkey, so they knew that some lands were hot. The different climates in this story may reflect their experiences.

In ancient times Ginnungagap, the Great Void, divided freezing Niflheim in the north from burning Muspell in the south. One day, a river flowed into Niflheim from the warm south. At once, its waters froze. More and more water flowed into Niflheim until a strong floor of ice was formed between the two lands. Where hot and cold met, the ice thawed and formed a frost giant called Ymir.

Ymir stood up and stretched. From one enormous arm dropped a giant; from the other, a giantess. From his feet came a son. The ice, still melting, created a cow, Andhumla. The four hungry giants saw four rivers of milk flowing from her udders. They drank deeply until their bellies were full. Andhumla was hungry too, by now. She licked the icy rocks and tasted salt.

'I like this,' she thought. 'I'll have some more.' As she licked, she saw some hair. The next day she licked some more. A head came through the rocks. On the

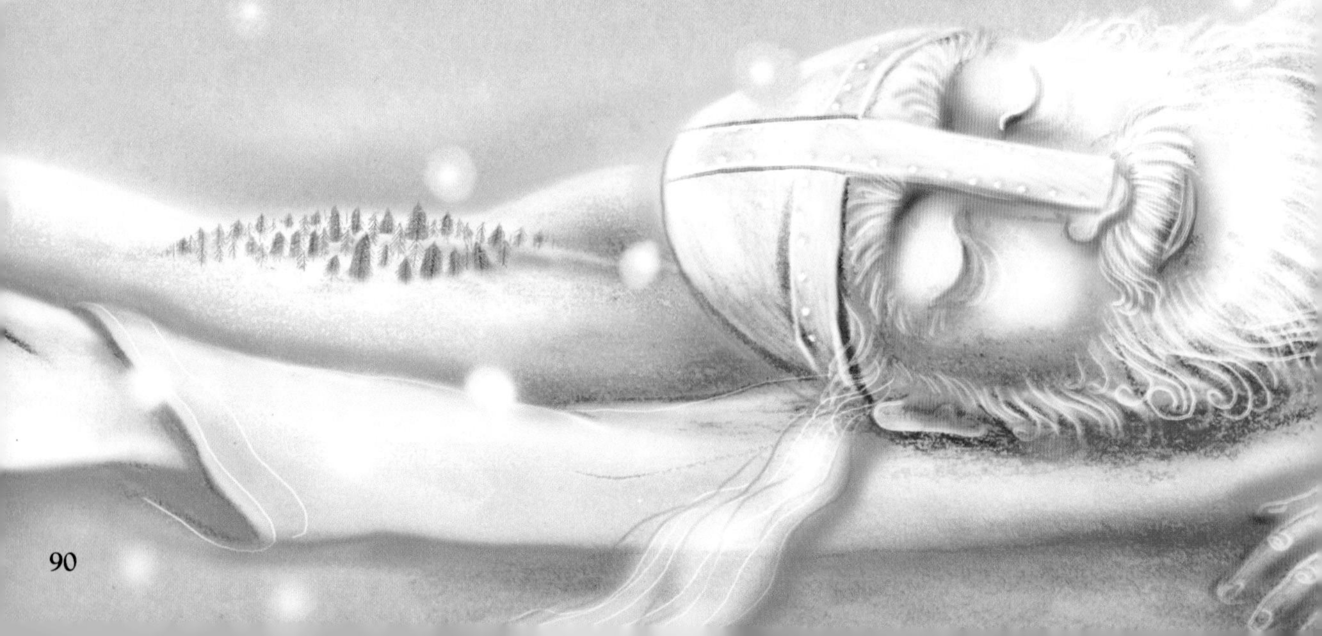

third day, a body appeared. It was the god Buri. He soon had a son, Bor, who married a giantess. They had three sons called Odin, Vili and Ve.

'Ymir makes the world too cold,' complained Odin one day. 'Help me get rid of him.' His brothers agreed.

From Ymir's blood, Odin made rivers and oceans.

'Now help me put his body in the Great Void,' he told his brothers. There, Ymir's flesh became the earth and his bones the mountains. Odin lifted Ymir's skull high and created the sky. To light it, he caught the sparks that flew all the way to Niflheim from the fires of Muspell and they became the stars and planets. From Ymir's brains, Odin made dark storm-clouds.

Odin and his family became the race of gods known as the Aesir. They lived in Asgard, Godland. One day as they walked along the seashore, they saw an ash tree and an elm tree and turned them into the first man and woman.

Odin and his brothers looked proudly at their work. There was just one more job to be done. Odin took Ymir's eyebrows and built a large wall.

'This will keep the giants out,' he said.

The land within the wall was known as Midgard, or Middle Earth, where the human race would eventually come to live.

Odin and the Tree of Life

Odin, the father of the Viking gods, travelled the world helping people, disguised as an old man in a hood which hid his face. He carried a spear called Gungnir and wore a ring called Draupnir. Odin's pet ravens, Hugin and Munnin, brought him marvellous stories from their journeys but Odin was not satisfied. He wanted the power to know everything.

ODIN DECIDED TO VISIT MIMIR'S SPRING IN SEARCH OF GREATER WISDOM. He leapt astride eight-legged Sleipnir – the swiftest horse in the world – and together they flew across Bifrost, the rainbow bridge which linked Asgard to the famous tree Yggdrasil, at the centre of the world.

Odin jumped off his horse and strode towards the spring, which gushed beneath Yggdrasil. But every time he put his mouth to the bubbling water, it ceased to flow.

'What's the drink worth to you?' laughed the giant Mimir, who guarded the spring.

'Whatever it takes,' Odin vowed.

'Something that is very dear to you,' Mimir replied.

Odin thought hard. 'My eyes,' he said at last. 'I will sacrifice one of my eyes to drink from your spring.' Mimir agreed. Odin put his mouth to the cool spring waters. When he had drunk long and deep, he looked around. Where were the runes, the symbols that contained all knowledge?

'You seek powerful magic, Odin,' Mimir's voice said. 'The runes come only to one who experiences death and lives again. Do you dare risk it?'

'I do.' Odin gazed up at Yggdrasil. Its windswept arms thrust against each other, inviting Odin up, challenging him. Odin began to climb. At the top of the tree, he wound his arms firmly around the branches. Now the wind could not dash him to the ground.

Fastened to the tree for nine days and nights, Odin was in agonies of thirst and starvation. He was so weak that his mind left

Yggdrasil, also known as the World Tree, was an enormous ash tree whose branches covered the world. Its three main roots led underground to Mimir's spring, the Well of Urd, the home of the three Norns or goddesses who planned human fate and to Niflheim, the realm of the dead. The runes which appeared by the tree (see page 94) were the first alphabet and a few wise people were able to predict the future from the way they were arranged.

his body and took him to places where he saw more with his one remaining eye than he had ever seen with two. He could hear secrets still inside the minds of those who thought them. He could move in an instant from one world to another.

'Living beings can't do this,' thought Odin. 'I must be dead. I've failed.'

The night that followed was long. Odin seemed to float above his body, watching it dangle, lifeless, in the branches of the tree. Then at last the rays of the rising sun made the world glitter. Now he would join the dead gods. But at least he would never again suffer the pain of the past nine days.

The next moment, a pain like a thunderbolt flashed through every part of Odin. He was back in his body! Far beneath him, by the foot of the tree, he could see strange strands of light flow into lines, triangles, knots.

'The runes!' Odin exclaimed. Swiftly he freed his arms and climbed down, gathering the glowing symbols to himself. Suddenly, he felt strong. It was the strength of someone who has known sacrifice, experienced death and in return acquired the greatest gift of all – the power of knowledge.

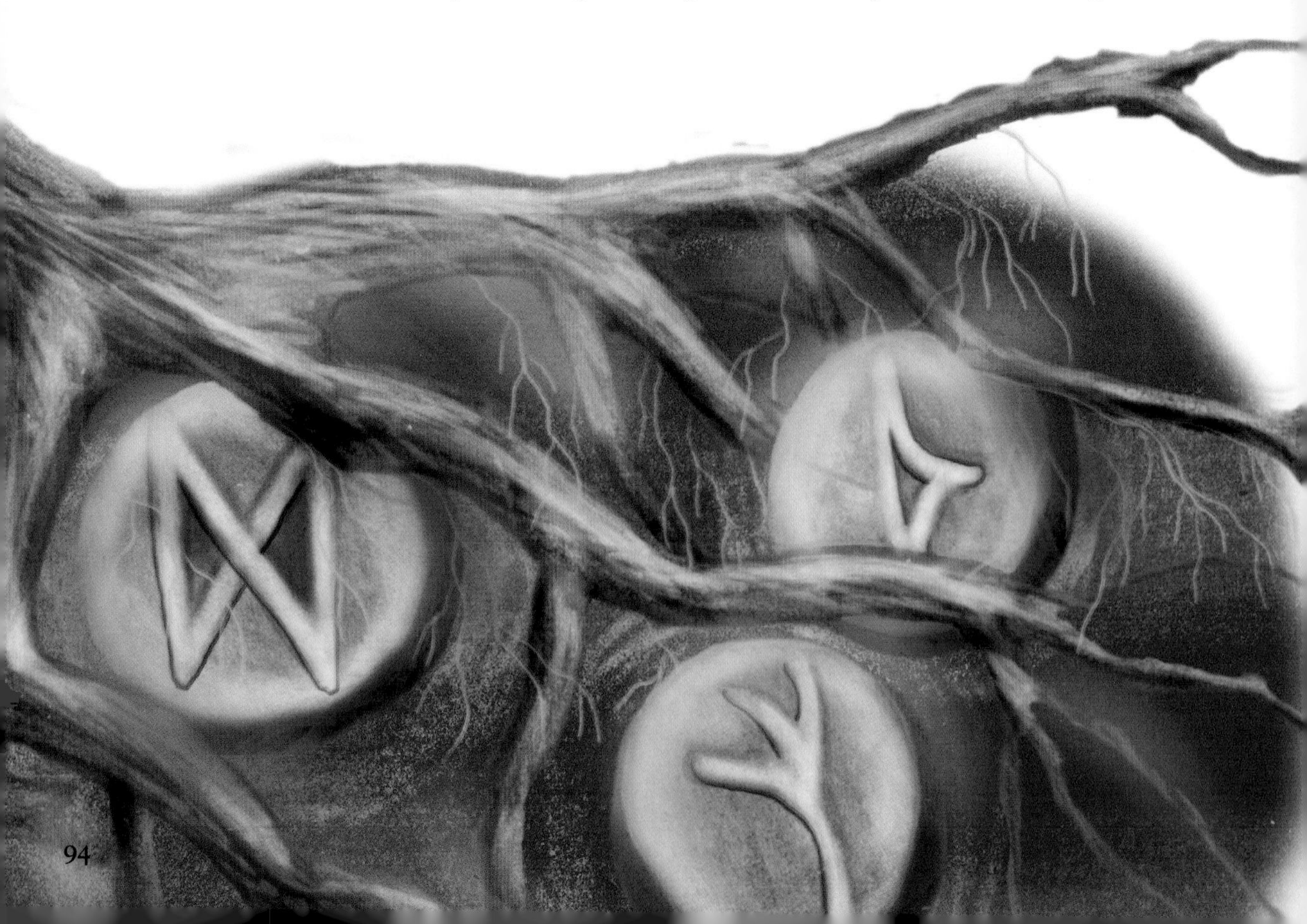

Viking Gods and Goddesses

The Aesir and the Vanir were the two groups of gods worshipped by the Vikings. When the Aesir first arrived in Scandinavia, they tried to take away the power of the Vanir. After fighting a war, they decided to live together. To ensure peace, they exchanged family members.

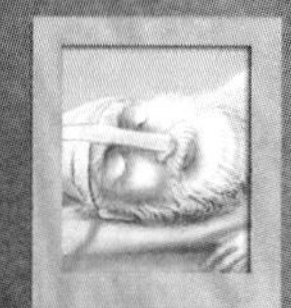

Ymir – the frost giant whose body formed the world

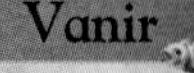

Vanir

Niord – god of the sea, fishing and treasure

Aesir

Bor – son of Buri, ancestor of the first gods

Frey – god of fertility, sunshine and rain

Freya – goddess of life, spring and growth, Frey's twin

Odin – ruler of the gods and god of mystery, magic and warriors. Wednesday is named after him

Frigg – goddess of humans, wife of Odin

Thor – god of the sky and a fierce warrior. Thursday is named after him

Heimdall – god of light and guardian of Bifrost, the rainbow bridge

Tyr – brave and wise god of war

Baldur – the shining god, son of Odin and Frigg

Hod – blind god of the night, Baldur's twin

Hermod – messenger to the gods

Loki – god of fire and trickster

Iormungand – the world serpent, son of Loki

Hel – ruler of the Underworld, daughter of Loki

Fenrir – fierce wolf, brother of Hel and Iormungand

Thor and the Giants

The early Vikings honoured the storm god Thor most of all because, like them, he was a warrior and made long journeys over harsh terrain. Thor fought for order against the giants who embodied chaos and that is why he was their greatest enemy. Thor's hammer, Miollnir, was the most powerful of all the gods' weapons. His worshippers used tiny models of it for luck.

Loki was the god of fire. He was a trickster god who helped the other gods but also got them into trouble to save himself. Loki had an evil side and the Vikings believed that he, along with his children, would destroy the world at Ragnarok *(see page 103).*

The Hammer of Thor

THOR OPENED HIS EYES, YAWNED AND REACHED FOR HIS TRUSTY HAMMER MIOLLNIR. It had vanished – stolen by the giants who were Thor's sworn enemies.

'The giants will destroy the gods and take over Asgard!' Thor bellowed to his friend Loki.

Loki nodded, troubled. 'Let's ask Freya for help.'

When Freya heard what had happened, she lent Loki her cloak of feathers. He soared high above the world, looking everywhere for the hammer. It was indeed in the land of the giants, which was also known as Iotunheim. A giant called Thrym had stolen it.

'Neither the gods of Aesir or Vanir can get it back,' bragged Thrym, 'unless Freya agrees to be my bride.'

Foolishly, Loki tried to persuade Freya to marry the giant. 'We'll rescue you as soon as Thrym gives back the hammer,' he assured her. But Freya was furious.

'How can you suggest such a thing?' she scolded him.

Loki narrowed his eyes. 'I have a better idea. Thor, you can pretend to be Freya!'

'I'm no woman!' thundered Thor, his great red beard bristling with the insult.

Even Freya had to laugh, imagining muscle-bound Thor in a bridal gown. 'Go on, Thor,' she giggled. 'It'll be worth it to get back Miollnir and save Asgard.'

Finally, Thor agreed. Freya dressed him in a fine veil and bridal gown and Loki escorted him to Iotunheim

where Thrym and his friends were enjoying the wedding feast.

'Here is Freya,' said Loki, seating the veiled Thor beside Thrym.

'What an enormous woman,' gasped Thrym.

'She is the great goddess of the Vanir,' Loki replied, trying not to smile. 'What did you expect? An elf?'

Thrym looked at his veiled bride wolfing down the wedding feast.

'She has a big appetite,' he remarked. 'And she's quite a drinker.'

'Ah!' sighed Loki, terrified that any moment now the game would be up. 'She's starved for love of you since the marriage was arranged.'

Flattered, Thrym gave the command Thor and Loki were waiting for.

'Bring the hammer to bless the bride!'

The hammer arrived and with a mighty roar, Thor seized it. The giants rose to attack him, but with Miollnir in his hand, Thor was invincible. The gods were safe again.

Thor and Iormungand

Thor was a fierce enemy of the World Serpent, Iormungand, who was the son of Loki and the giantess Angrboda. Iormungand coiled himself around the world, lurking in the mighty ocean which surrounded Yggdrasil. The Vikings believed that Thor and Iormungand would finally confront and destroy one another at Ragnarok.

ONCE A GIANT GAVE THOR SHELTER FOR THE NIGHT.

'Is it really you the Aesir boast about?' he mocked. 'You don't look fit to lift that old cat.'

Thor was insulted. He looked over at the limp creature and his cheeks blazed with fury. He grabbed the cat but it did not budge. Thor tried again. Still, it did not move. Soon, he was huffing and puffing.

'It's as heavy as a mountain,' he thought, giving it a final heave. The cat swung off the ground.

'Put it down, I beg you,' the giant pleaded.

Thor saw he was sweating with fear. 'What's the matter?' he asked, puzzled.

'That was no cat,' the giant confessed. 'It was Iormungand. Please let him go or the world will end.'

Thor reluctantly let go but he hadn't forgotten his rival. Soon he was able to challenge him again when he visited the home of a giant called Hymir.

'I'm going fishing,' Hymir announced rudely. 'You have to leave.'

'Why? I'll go fishing with you,' Thor replied.

Hymir laughed. 'You won't be able to stand the sea chill. You should stay on land.'

But Thor insisted, so Hymir told him to find some bait. Thor strode out and returned with a large ox's head. They both got into Hymir's boat and Thor started rowing vigorously.

'Stop,' Hymir said. 'The fishing is good here.'

Thor rowed on. 'We're getting close to Iormungand's territory,' Hymir warned.

Still Thor rowed on until they reached the centre of the ocean. With one throw, he flung out his line, baited with the ox-head. He felt a tug on his reel. Iormungand had taken the bait, but the fishing hook had lodged in his jaw and he thrashed about wildly, making Thor's hand smash against the side of the boat. Thor stamped down in pain. His feet went through the boat's bottom and hit the sea-bed. Instantly, Iormungand attacked, spitting venom in Thor's face. Thor reached for his hammer but before he could throw it, Hymir cut the reel and set Iormungand free. Once again, a giant had saved him from mighty Thor.

In this story, Geirrod and his daughters Gialp and Greip represent the uncontrollable forces of nature such as floods, earthquakes and volcanic eruptions which the Vikings had to overcome, in order to survive. They saw Thor as their protector against the chaos of nature.

Geirrod and his daughters

THE GIANT GEIRROD HAD INVITED THOR TO VISIT HIM IN IOTUNHEIM, BUT HE INSISTED THOR LEFT HIS INSTRUMENTS OF POWER BEHIND. 'He's up to something,' Thor thought, setting off to find out.

The journey was long and as night fell, Thor saw a hut and stopped to ask if he could spend the night there. A friendly giantess welcomed him in.

'Geirrod is a fierce fellow,' she said the next morning, learning of his purpose. 'Take these to help you.' She gave him a belt, a walking stick and some iron gloves. Thor thanked her and continued on his way.

Soon he came to the heaving river, Vimur. Thor put on his belt and started to wade across. Instantly, the waters rose until they reached his chin but the belt somehow kept him afloat. In the distance, stood Geirrod's daughter Gialp, grinning. Thor hurled a rock at her. Gialp fell back and Thor swam to safety across the river.

When he arrived at Geirrod's door he was sent to a shabby little hut. Thor slumped into the only chair in the room. This was no place for a guest and Thor would tell Geirrod so when he saw him. Suddenly, the chair wobbled under Thor and flew upwards. He felt his mighty body crushed against the ceiling. Thor thrust his stick hard against the rafters. Instantly, they smashed and the chair fell down with a crash. Gialp and her sister Greip fell to either side, shrieking and wailing. They had been under the chair!

Geirrod heard their screams. It was time to face Thor himself.

'You want a fight, Geirrod?' Thor roared, stepping into the giant's hall. 'Well, you'll get one.' As Thor raged, Geirrod hurled a brick of molten iron at him. Thor held up his hands, clad in the iron gloves. The brick flew back at Geirrod, crashing through a pillar, smashing the giant's skull and pushing him through a wall.

'That's what happens to giants who try to kill their guests!' Thor bellowed as he turned and strode furiously back to Asgard.

Tyr, the bravest God

Fenrir the wolf was one of the three children of Loki and Angrboda. When Odin was warned that Loki's children would destroy the world, he flung Iormungand into the sea and banished Hel to the Underworld. Here is how the gods dealt with Fenrir.

FENRIR SNARLED AND SNAPPED, STRAINING AGAINST THE CHAIN WITH WHICH THE GODS HAD BOUND HIM.

'He gets stronger every day,' laughed Loki, his father. But the other gods didn't join in. They had bound the fearsome wolf with countless strong chains, but every time he broke free. The Aesir decided to go to the dwarves. They were clever craftsmen and would know how to help.

'We will make a chain of six elements,' promised the dwarves. 'The lurking of a cat, the breath of a fish, the saliva of a bird, the muscles of a bear, the beard of a woman and the core of a mountain.'

When the chain was ready, the gods took it to

Fenrir. 'Can you break this chain?' they asked.

Fenrir laughed at the flimsy cord. 'Are you trying to insult me?' he snarled. 'A worm could snap that piece of string.'

Then he narrowed his eyes. 'Unless it is some cunning magic? I want nothing to do with magic.'

'Poor Fenrir,' the gods mocked. 'Look how frightened he is of this frail chain.'

They mocked and teased until Fenrir agreed to be bound. But he had one condition. 'Throughout the contest, the hand of one god must remain in my mouth.'

The gods all fell silent. But Tyr, the mighty god of war, stepped forward and bravely put his hand in Fenrir's mouth. Swiftly, another god slipped the magic chain around the wolf's neck.

The contest began. Fenrir thrashed his neck from side to side, trying to break the chain. His jaws frothed and his coat grew dark with sweat. Tyr did not flinch.

At last, Fenrir realised he had been tricked. With a howl of fury, he clamped his teeth around Tyr's wrist, and bit off his hand. Brave Tyr did not utter a word as the other gods rushed over to seize Fenrir. They slipped a sword between the wolf's teeth to stop him biting, then tethered him to a large rock.

'And there you shall stay until the world's end,' declared Odin.

The word Ragnarok means twilight or doom of the gods. According to the Voluspa, written around 1000 CE, at Ragnarok Fenrir will break his chains and his snarling jaws will open wide enough to reach from heaven to hell. Iormungand will raise a mighty tidal wave. A boat captained by Loki will carry the fire giant Surt of Muspell to a battle with the god Frey. Surt will defeat Frey and burn the world to a cinder.

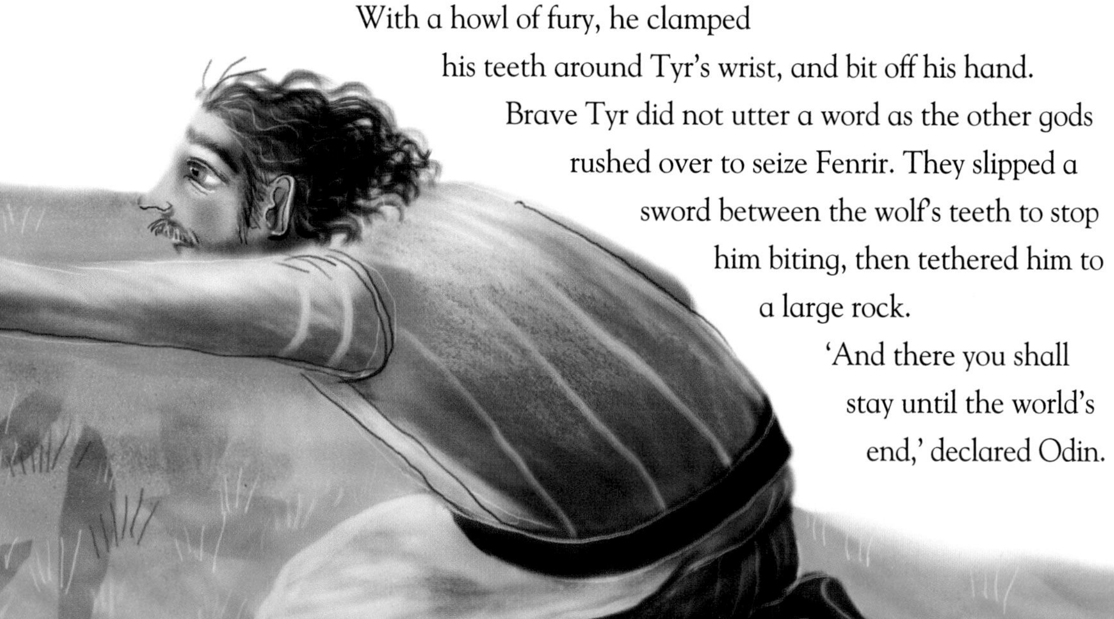

Baldur, the Shining God

Most mythologies have a story in which a young god or goddess is trapped in the world of the dead. This was how ancient people explained summer and winter. Baldur, young and radiant, is like the sun in summer. His absence darkens the world and brings on winter. This story also tells us that the Vikings believed in life after death.

ODIN'S SON, BALDUR WAS HAVING NIGHTMARES. Odin was very worried about him. He decided to visi an oracle who could tell him Baldur's future.

'Hel's people await Baldur,' the oracle told Odin.

Greatly saddened, Odin returned to his wife Frigg and told her of the oracle's words.

'But everyone loves Baldur,' said Frigg. 'Who would want to kill him?'

Odin shook his head. 'She would not say.'

Frigg travelled the earth, asking all living things to promise they would not harm Baldur. The air, the plants, the mountains and waters, all gave her their word. Baldur would never die – neither poison nor metal nor disease would harm him. To prove it, the gods invented a game. They hurled all kinds of things at Baldur but nothing could hurt him.

Loki was jealous of the young, handsome god. 'Baldur is more popular than ever,' he grumbled. 'I have to put an end to it.' Loki disguised himself as an old woman and visited Frigg.

'Is it true that every animal, mineral and vegetable made this promise?' he asked.

'All but a tiny mistletoe near Valhalla. It was too young to understand,' Frigg whispered.

Loki could hardly contain his glee. He flew to Valhalla, ripped out the mistletoe and returned to Asgard where the gods were playing their favourite game. A little apart from the rest stood Hod, Baldur's twin.

'Why aren't you joining in?' Loki asked.

'You know quite well I'm blind,' Hod said.

'Be a sport for once,' Loki said. He thrust the mistletoe into Hod's hand and directed his throw. The mistletoe pierced Baldur and he fell to the ground, dead. As the gods and goddesses mourned, Loki fled.

The gods placed Baldur on his longboat along with many treasures. As the boat burst into flames, the god Hermod leapt on Sleipner's back and crossed Gioll, the long river to the Underworld.

The ancient Viking festival of Yuletide was celebrated to lure back the sun, Baldur. The Vikings kept a tree trunk burning for twelve days and hung decorations on evergreen trees. These two traditions are still found at Christmas-time all over the Christian world.

'Set Baldur free,' he told the goddess Hel. 'All living things weep for him.'

'Then let their tears wash him out of the Underworld,' she replied scornfully.

Hermod immediately sent out Hel's message. Every living creature wept for Baldur, except a giantess called Thokki, who jeered: 'Let Hel keep him.'

And so Baldur remained in the Land of the Dead. But the gods suspected that Thokki was Loki in disguise. They tied him to three rocks where he will stay until the end of the world.

Sigurd's Quest

This story is from Volsungsaga, a 13th century Scandinavian saga telling of King Volsung of Hunland and his son Sigmund, a famous hero of Viking mythology. A saga is a tale spanning many generations. The third part of Volsungsaga follows the adventures of Sigmund's son, Sigurd, another Viking hero.

PRINCE SIGURD WAS HAPPY LIVING IN THE KINGDOM OF DENMARK UNDER THE PROTECTION OF THE KING. The court swordsmith, Regin, was busy teaching him all that a young prince needed to know of fighting and travelling and wisdom and Sigurd was an eager pupil.

One day Regin told Sigurd about a great hoard of treasure that lay in a cave guarded by the monster Fafnir. 'You should kill him and seize the treasure,' Regin urged.

Sigurd agreed, full of enthusiasm. Regin prepared a sword for his quest. But when Sigurd practised using his new sword, its blade fell apart. Regin made another sword, and this time too the blade shattered.

Sigurd remembered his mother had saved the pieces of his father's sword which was said to be unconquerable. He gave them to Regin, who melted them down and crafted a sword strong enough to slice through metal and sharp enough to cut through string in a flowing river.

Sigurd was impatient to begin his adventure. 'Can I borrow a horse to go on a quest?' he asked the king.

'Choose one from my stable,' the king replied.

Sigurd eyed the horses in awe. They were all magnificent. How could he choose?

'What about this one?' a voice suggested. Sigurd turned to see a hooded stranger.

It was Odin in disguise. He pointed to a lively stallion, Grani, the son of his own horse Sleipnir. Sigurd wasted no time. He mounted Grani and rode off with Regin. At last they arrived at a cave hidden deep in the mountains. Regin pointed to the ground. 'See those footprints? Fafnir has gone to have a drink. Dig a trench on this path. When Fafnir returns, strike at his belly from below and kill him.'

As Sigurd was digging, the hooded stranger appeared again. 'The monster's blood is poisonous,' he warned. 'Dig some pits beside your trench. Then the blood will flow away without harming you.'

'Strange,' thought Sigurd, 'Regin never warned me about Fafnir's blood.' Again, he did as Odin advised and jumped out of the way as soon as he had struck the monster. Regin reappeared as Fafnir's blood drained into the pits. He put his hand to the monster's wound and pulled out its heart while Sigurd looked on in disgust. 'Roast this,' Regin commanded. 'I will return later to eat it.' Sigurd built a fire and skewered the monster's heart to the spit.

The dwarves in Viking myths are clever craftsmen who can make magical objects. They brewed a special drink known as mead which turned its drinker into a poet. They also created Thor's hammer. Their most incredible creation was a gold ring belonging to Odin called Draupnir, which reproduced itself every nine days.

The heart sizzled and frothed as it cooked over the flames and its hot juice spattered on to Sigurd's thumb. Sigurd sucked hard at it to stop the searing pain. Suddenly, he realised that he could understand the language of the birds. They were talking about him!

'Poor Sigurd doesn't realise that Regin's really a monster,' twittered one bird.

'Do you think he'll kill Sigurd once he's got his hands on the gold?' asked his companion.

'Why not?' replied the first bird. 'He killed his father for it – and his brother.'

The birds discussed how the god Loki, out hunting, had accidentally shot Regin's brother, Otter. Regin's father had demanded a ransom of gold from Loki which the god had cunningly tricked out of a dwarf. Regin killed his father for the gold, but then found that his other brother, Fafnir, had taken it.

'Sigurd should kill him first and take the gold. Then he can ride to the Hinderfiall Mountains to rescue the brave warrior that no one else can save,' decided the bird.

Sigurd could not believe his ears. Regin had pretended to be his friend so that he could kill him and take the gold. Now Sigurd was forced to kill or be killed, so he chopped off Regin's head, seized the gold and rode off in search of the Hinderfiall Mountains.

As he neared the mountains, he saw a bright flickering light before him, leaping and dancing.

'Come on my friend,' he said to Grani, 'let's jump through it.' With a mighty bound Grani brought Sigurd through the fire and into a courtyard held up

The Valkyries were daughters of Odin. They were warrior women who helped Odin's favourite heroes and kings in battle. They carried heroes killed in war to Valhalla, where Odin ruled the heroic dead. Valhalla was different from Hel, the Land of the Dead, where the old and sick went after dying. Heroes will live happily in Valhalla until Ragnarok when they will rise and fight against the evil forces of Loki and his three children.

by stone pillars. In its centre lay a fully armed warrior.

Sigurd walked slowly up to the still figure, every bit of it covered in armour. Who could it be?

Sigurd pulled his sword Gram from his belt and ran its point round the helmet. The armour fell away, revealing a beautiful young woman dressed in white.

The woman sat up. 'My name is Brynhild,' she told Sigurd. 'I am a Valkyrie. I help heroes in battle.'

Brynhild explained that Odin had told her to help a warrior called Helmut Gunnar win a battle. But between battles, she had turned herself into a swan and, as she swam, one of Helmut's enemies had stolen her clothes. 'He refused to return them unless I helped him. So Helmut lost the battle and Odin punished my disobedience by putting me to sleep here in a ring of fire. He said that unless a hero came who was brave enough to leap through the fire, I would lie here forever.'

Sigurd was delighted he had saved Brynhild. From that day on, many called him the 'Fire-walker'.

TALES FROM INDIAN MYTHS

INTRODUCTION

Indian myths are mostly about the constant war between good and evil. They also teach that it is important to worship the gods and that everything in nature is cyclical. In its early history, India was often invaded and this is reflected in the two great epics, the Ramayana and the Mahabharata. The sources of Indian stories are many, but they are hard to date. The Rigveda, which tells us about the early nature gods, Indra and his family, was complied between 1500 and 900 BCE. The Ramayana is thought to have been composed around 1000 BCE, and the Mahabharata a hundred years later in 900 BCE. The myths exist in many different Indian languages and leave a vivd account of the way of life in India across a long time-span. The religious beliefs set out in the books are still practised today.

The early Indian gods were nature gods. The ancient Indians made offerings to them so that they would be rewarded with plenty of water and sun to bring good harvests. These people often travelled huge distances, looking for new lands to settle. They took their own gods and myths with them on their journeys. When they settled somewhere new, an exchange took place. They introduced their gods to the local people and, in turn, began to worship some of theirs. So over time more myths were added to each story-telling tradition, and sometimes the same gods were called different names as old stories blended with new ones. In India, Indra, the supreme god of the prehistoric Indians, lost much of his importance over time. He was replaced by the new god of the fields and hillsides, Krishna. Their rivalry in myths such as the lifting of Govardhan (see page 123) shows how the worshippers of the new gods believed their own gods to be superior. On the other hand, another prehistoric god, Brahma, was easily absorbed into the new family of Indian gods where he worked alongside Vishnu, as we see in the myth of the recreation of the world. Over the centuries, the new gods gained prominence and the female divine, Shakti, became more widely worshipped, particularly in the warlike form of Kali.

The Cosmic Ocean

This story describes how two of the best-known Indian gods, Brahma and Vishnu, remake the cosmos again and again. Hindus believe people are continually reborn in other forms, so death is a stage of life, not the end. The world is also continually recreated in the same way.

Vasuki was the king of the serpents, who were demi-gods and lived in the dark underworld, known as Patal. Cobras are still respected all over India and on one day of the year, Nag Panchami, saucers of milk are left out to feed them. Vasuki is also known as Shesh Nag.

THE GREAT GOD VISHNU, PRESERVER OF THE UNIVERSE, SURVEYED THE WORLD. All seemed peaceful.

'It is time to rest,' Vishnu decided, raising his hand to summon Vasuki, chief of the serpents. Vasuki arrived, dressed in magnificent robes of purple, wearing rows of glimmering white pearls, and offered his wide back as a bed to the god. Vishnu lay down on Vasuki's back and the great cobra spread his thousand hoods to shade the god as he prepared to float on the Cosmic Ocean.

Vishnu sank into a deep sleep that would last the whole night. But one night of the gods is many millennia for humans. And while Vishnu slept, the whole universe was destroyed and recreated. It began as Vasuki spat out a special poison which turned into a fire, which made the universe slowly burn and sink into the Cosmic Ocean.

But Brahma, the god of creation, was ready. He placed a golden seed in the swirling waters of the Ocean and waited for it to grow into an egg. When the egg hatched, Brahma himself emerged from it and sat on a lotus flower in the centre to create the new cosmos. He raised one half of the egg and made it the sky. The second half, he placed beneath him, creating the Earth. The golden yolk in the centre became the radiant sun, Surya.

When Vishnu finally stirred and awoke, he would discover a whole new cosmos and his work for the day would begin again.

The Birth of Indra

Ancient Indians claimed they did not know how the world began, only that Dyaus-Pitar (Sky), and his wife Prithvi (Earth), created the nature gods. These included Ushas (dawn) and Vayu (wind), but also Vritra, the serpent of drought and famine. The fight between Vritra and Indra in this myth represents the eternal struggle of farming communities against the harsh forces of nature.

THE PLANTS AND FIELDS HAD WITHERED AWAY. It made Prithvi, the Earth, sad and angry.

'Vritra is taking away the water from the world,' she told Dyaus-Pitar, the Sky. 'We must stop him.'

She blinked and suddenly, two young men lay sleeping before her. One sat up. He had four arms. One arm held a sword, a second wielded Vajra, his thunderbolt-spear, and the third, a rainbow with which t shoot arrows. His fourth arm was free to be used when h faced Vritra, the serpent of drought and famine.

'This is our son Indra,' Prithvi smiled at Dyaus-Pita 'He is master of the atmosphere and protector of harvest His sleeping brother is Agni, god of fire.'

Before confronting Vritra, Indra went first to the nature spirits, known as the Gandharvas, who made him soma – a magical juice which gave its drinkers enormous strength.

Indra drank the juice until he felt power course through his body. Then he leapt on his chariot and soared through the skies on his mission. Vritra had hidden himself in distant fortresses made of clouds and mist, but Indra was not put off. He destroyed one fortress after another until, at last, he cornered Vritra.

The fearsome serpent snarled and lunged at him. But Indra was ready. He crouched until Vritra was close, then flung Vajra vigorously. Vritra gave a great roar. His belly split, releasing the waters of Earth, which flooded out into the clouds and cascaded down to Earth. At last, years of drought and famine came to an end. The land grew lush, crops flourished and people could eat again. Vritra lived on in the skies, threatening to bring drought another day. But Indra would always be ready for him.

This story is from the Rigveda, a book of hymns compiled between 1500-900 BCE. Its gods symbolise nature and are called the Vedic gods. The three most important were Indra, god of fertility and rain, Surya, the Sun, and Indra's twin, Agni, who was fire. All three were worshipped by ancient Indians who lived off the land.

The Churning of the Ocean of Milk

The Indian gods fought a constant battle with the demons. The demons devoted years of prayer to gain powers to use against the gods. The god Shiva insisted the prayers of worshippers, even evil ones, had to be rewarded. So the world was always in danger from these evil creatures.

INDRA, KING OF THE GODS, WAS GROWING WEAK. 'We need Vishnu's help to make him stronger,' the anxious gods decided. 'If we fail, the demons will triumph and make the world an evil place.'

The gods set off for Vaikuntha, Vishnu's heaven.

'The Elixir of Life will increase your strength fourfold,' Vishnu told Indra. 'To get it, you must churn the Ocean of Milk. Use Vasuki, king of the serpents, as a rope. Mount Mandan will be your churning stick. You will pull from one side and the demons from the other.'

'The demons?' Indra gasped. 'But we can't let them have the elixir. They'll become even stronger!'

Vishnu chuckled. 'You need their strength. I will make sure they don't drink the elixir.'

The gods and the demons gathered around the Ocean of Milk. Each side held firmly onto Vasuki and pulled. The mountain swivelled from side to side. The ocean waves rose, making the milky water froth and foam. Faster and faster they pulled, as if in a tug of war. The mountain spun so furiously, it bored deep into the ground. Vishnu turned a part of himself into a large tortoise and stood beneath the mountain to hold up the world. As the churning continued, a cow appeared from the foaming surface of the ocean.

'This is Surabhi, the cow of plenty,' Vishnu said. 'She can grant all wishes.' As the gods helped Surabhi out, the ocean turned into a frothing whirlpool.

There were many demon races - Asuras, Daityas and Danavas. They included giants and ogres, as well as goblins, vampires and ghosts, and their aim was to take over the world and destroy all the good in it. They worshipped Shiva, god of destruction, the third god of the triad of Brahma, Vishnu and Shiva.

Best known today as Shiva, this god was also known as Rudra in the Rigveda. He wears his hair in a top-knot decorated with the crescent moon and smears his body in ashes as a sign of his religious nature. Shiva also wears a necklace of skulls, and is often linked to the dead. But Shiva is the god of creation, as well as destruction. He ensures that everything is reborn after dying.

One by one, miraculous creatures and objects emerged from the frothy water. First came the Apsaras, heavenly dancing maidens. The goddess of good fortune, Lakshmi, appeared and Vishnu decided to take her as a wife. The crescent moon flew out and attached itself to Shiva's hair. Then came poison, which Shiva swallowed before the demons could reach it. It stained his throat deep blue.

At last, an old physician rose to the surface. He was holding up a chalice which contained the Elixir of Life! The demons and the gods rushed to get to it first. But the demons were stronger and surged together towards the physician. Suddenly, they heard exquisite music. The Apsaras were dancing. The demons were enchanted.

The next moment, the gods had taken possession of the chalice. Vishnu had kept his promise to take care of the demons and Indra's strength was restored.

Vedic and Hindu Gods

The gods of Indian myths can be divided into the old gods who come from the Vedas, and the new Hindu gods who rose to popularity later and remain dominant to this day.

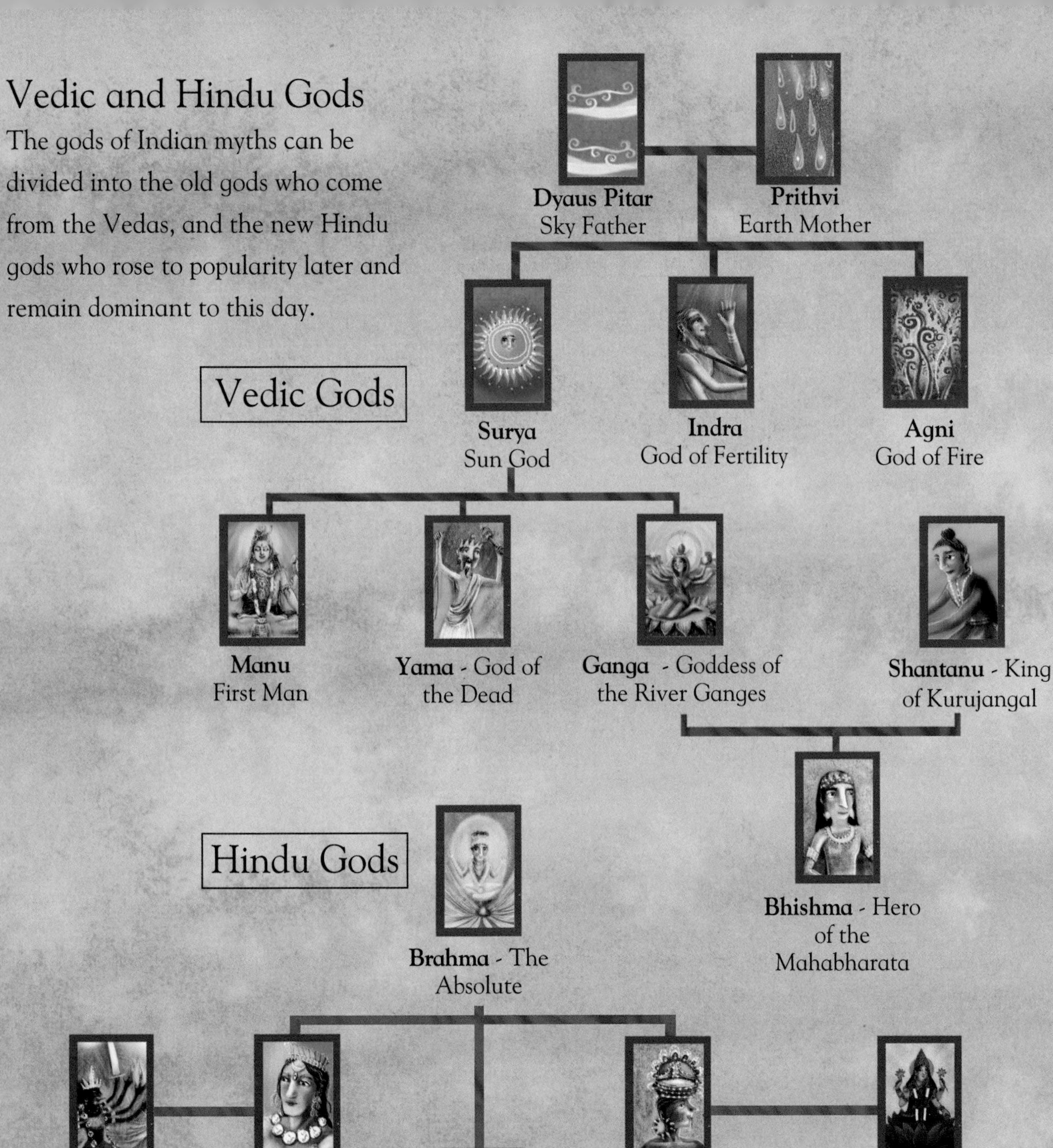

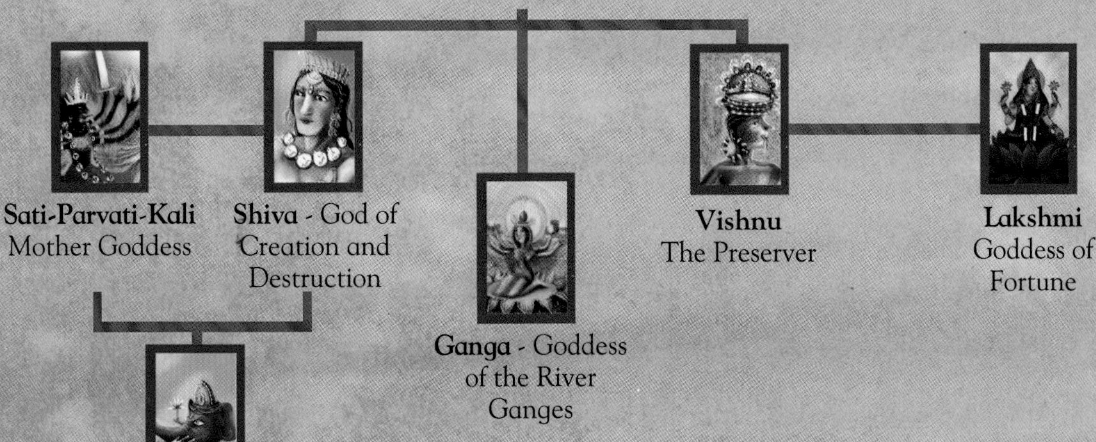

Krishna, God of the Fields

This story of the birth of Krishna comes from a book called the Bhagavada Purana, which is believed to have been written around 1000 CE. Krishna, the flute-player, is one of the most popular Hindu gods. Songs are still sung all over India about his antics as a naughty child, getting milkmaids into trouble by drinking their milk and eating up their freshly churned butter.

Krishna was the blue-grey of a rain cloud. This was probably because he took over the role of bringing rain and keeping the fields fertile from Indra. As a god, he wore a gold necklace and a crown decorated with a peacock feather.

KING KANS OF MATHURA WAS AN EVIL SORCERER AND A CRUEL KING.

One day, he summoned his guards to him.

'Imprison my sister Devaki and her husband Vasudev,' he ordered. 'My magic tells me that their eighth son will kill me and take away my kingdom.'

Devaki and Vasudev were locked into their home and, one by one, Devaki's sons were killed at birth. Only the seventh, Balrama, was saved because Vasudev managed to spirit him away to a distant village.

The great god Vishnu was watching over King Kans with disapproval. 'It is time to deal with Kans,' he decided. 'I will be reborn as his eighth child.'

Devaki soon gave birth to an eighth son, named Krishna. She and Vasudev gazed at their new-born baby, terrified that he too would soon be taken from them. But instead, Vishnu appeared before them, large and glowing.

'Take baby Krishna to the village of Gokul,' Vishnu ordered Vasudev. 'Exchange him for the new-born daughter of Yashodha and Nand Lal, the cowherd. King Kans has no reason to kill Devaki's daughter.'

Vasudev looked grimly at the chains on the door, but they fell away before his eyes and he walked through. Soon he arrived at the river Jamuna, which raged wildly, making it impossible to cross. Suddenly, a path appeared among the stormy waters before him. Clutching Krishna to him, Vasudev made his way to the cowherd's house.

Here, Vishnu helped out again. 'Vasudev will leave Krishna the child god for you to look after,' he told Yashodha and Nand. 'In return, your daughter will live with Vasudev and his wife Devaki like a princess.'

When Vishnu had gone, Yashodha and Nand forgot everything and believed Krishna to be their own son.

Krishna grew up in the countryside and the people from all around loved him dearly. He encouraged them to worship the god Vishnu instead of Indra, the protector of harvests. This infuriated Indra, who brought a rainstorm to punish the people. But Krishna lifted the huge mountain Govardhan and held it over the fields to shield their crops from the rain.

Kali, the Demon-slayer

Kali was a form of the mother goddess, Parvati, who was married to Shiva. The two gods often had contests with each other. This story of Kali in her most ferocious form is one of the best-known Indian myths. It tells us how Kali came to be created.

THE GIANTS SUMBHA AND NISUMBHA HAD WORSHIPPED SHIVA FOR MANY CENTURIES AND, IN RETURN FOR THEIR PRAYERS, HAD GAINED GREAT POWER.

'They boast they'll take over the world,' the gods grumbled to Shiva. 'You must reduce their force.'

'I will do no such thing,' said Shiva. 'They have earned their reward. But you could ask Parvati for help. She is, after all, the Cosmic Mother.'

Parvati agreed to help. She protected the world and would not let any giants take it over, even if they were Shiva's devotees.

Parvati climbed to the highest peak of the Himalayan mountains and took the form of Durga, a beautiful woman riding a lion. The armies of Sumbha and Nisumbha saw Durga and attacked. But Durga was too powerful and cut them down almost instantly. The giants realised they were up against a huge force. They sent out their best general, Raktavij, against Durga, accompanied by his army of giants. Durga grew enormous and swirled her ten arms, holding many magical weapons. Soon Raktavij's warriors lay strewn on the ground and he was fighting Durga alone. But every time she attacked Raktavij, a thousand warriors sprang from each drop of his blood that touched the ground.

'Kali!' Durga called. Instantly, a massive black goddess emerged from her body and stood beside her. As Durga fought Raktavij, Kali caught the drops of his blood in her mouth, stopping them from turning into warriors. Soon, Raktavij was dead. Sumbha and Nisumbha were dead too. Kali stood amid the slain demons, wild with triumph. She stamped her feet and started turning. The world became a drum beneath her feet, beating out a victory tattoo. The gods and goddesses clapped. Urged on by the praise, Kali danced more wildly. Her energy made the world shake. The cries of praise turned to shouts of warning, but Kali danced on.

Shiva knew he had to intervene. He lay down among the dead demons. When Kali brought her foot down beside him, she felt Shiva's energy. With a shock, Kali stopped her wild dance. She realised she had saved the world from the giants, but had nearly destroyed it herself through pride.

The name Parvati means 'daughter of the mountain'. This goddess is worshipped as Durga by warriors, and as Kali and in her other fierce forms by those wishing to drive away fear and evil. She was first born as Sati, or Truth, to teach the world, but when her father insulted Shiva, she vanished into a fire and returned many centuries later as the goddess Parvati. She is much loved throughout India.

Ganesh

Ganesh is widely worshipped in India and by Hindus all over the world. He is the god of wisdom, and sacrifices are offered to him at the beginning of new projects because he is the remover of obstacles. He is plump and yellow-skinned and his carriage is drawn by a rat. There are many stories explaining why Ganesh has the head of an elephant.

THE GOD SHIVA AND HIS BEAUTIFUL WIFE PARVATI LIVED HIGH UP IN THE HIMALAYAN MOUNTAINS.

The two gods loved each other deeply, but Shiva spent much of his time praying and meditating far away from home, and Parvati was often lonely.

One hot day Parvati decided to bathe in a nearby lake. She swam vigorously, stretching out her arms and legs. As she swam, the dust from her body mixed with the water and formed a baby. Parvati scooped the infant into her arms. She was delighted! Now she had a companion, and when Shiva eventually returned from his meditations, they would be a family.

Parvati took the baby home, lay down with him in her arms and fell asleep gazing at him in wonder. But the baby, Ganesh, was no ordinary infant. As soon as he saw his mother asleep, he crept out of bed and over to the door to guard her bed chamber.

Soon, Shiva completed his meditations and strode back over the mountains to see his wife.

The little boy god barred his way. 'Who are you?' he asked.

Shiva was furious. Who was this small stranger to question him?

'Get out of my way,' he commanded.

But Ganesh raised his arm and held Shiva back. Shiva could not stand to be insulted, even by a little boy. With a mighty blow, he struck off Ganesh's head and marched in to his wife's bedroom.

'What have you done?' Parvati screamed. 'That was your son!'

'Did he not know I am the great Lord of Creation and Destruction?' Shiva bellowed furiously.

'How could he know?' wept Parvati. 'He was only just born.'

Instantly, Shiva was sorry for what he had done. He summoned his messengers, the demons, goblins, witches and sprites of Earth and air.

'Find a head for my son,' Shiva ordered.

Everywhere Shiva's creatures looked, they saw infants asleep, facing their mothers and they could not bear to behead them. At last, they found a baby elephant who had turned his back to his mother because his trunk was in the way. Immediately, they took his head and Shiva fixed it to Ganesh's body. The little god sat up, alive again. And that is how Ganesh came to have the head of an elephant.

The great sage Vyasa wanted to dictate a book to Ganesh, who agreed on the condition that Vyasa told his story without a single pause. The sage dictated 90,000 verses of 30 lines each. This book became the great epic known as the Mahabharata – the longest poem in the world. Because of this, many Indian writers pray to Ganesh at the start of each new book.

The Great War

This story comes from the beginning of the epic poem the Mahabharata, (The Great War). It tells the story of the war between the one hundred Kauravas and their cousins, the five Pandavas, over who would rule the kingdom of Kurujangal. Bhishma is the most important character of the epic, because he is present from start to finish as the protector of the hundred Kauravas.

KING SHANTANU PULLED UP HIS WEARY HORSE BY THE RIVER GANGES. The river's pure waters would soothe his tiredness. As he splashed his face, he heard a tinkling noise and saw a beautiful woman bathing in the water. She wore a blue sari and glittering jewels and she was bathed in a strange glow.

'Who are you?' Shantanu asked.

'I am not of your world,' the woman replied.

But Shantanu was enchanted.

'Please marry me,' he begged.

'I will marry you,' the woman responded. 'But if you ever question my actions, I will leave you forever.'

Shantanu agreed to this condition and the entire kingdom celebrated the royal marriage. Soon, the queen gave birth to a son. Immediately, she walked to the window and hurled the baby into the rushing waters of the Ganges, saying, 'I do this for your own good.'

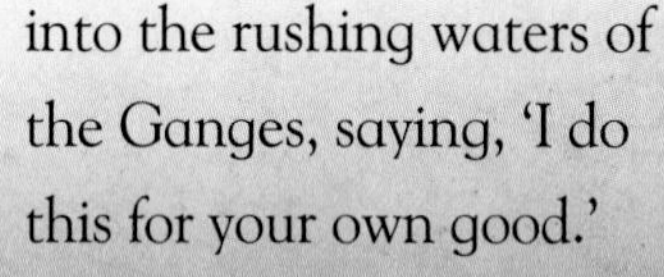

Shantanu was shattered, but he kept his promise. Six more times, the queen bore a boy and each time she fed it to the river with the same words. But when the eighth son came, Shantanu seized him from his mother's arms.

'Not this time,' he said. 'This son will live.'

'We could have been happy together with this son,' replied the queen sadly. 'But you have broken your promise and now I must go.'

Shantanu was heartbroken. 'Will you at least explain to me why you killed our sons?'

'I am Ganga, goddess of the river. The seven storm-gods were once cursed to be reborn as mortals. I could not prevent the curse, but I promised to release them from the cycle of rebirth. So I gave birth to each one and killed him before he sinned. Sinless and washed in my waters, they won't be reborn. This child is your heir. Call him Bhishma.'

Some say that the goddess Ganga sprang from the toe of Vishnu, while others claim that she was the daughter of Brahma. The story tells that she came down to Earth in the shape of the river Ganga (Ganges in English) because a king prayed for her to purify the wrong-doings of his ancestors. The Ganga is said to wash away the sins of her worshippers, even today.

When the five Pandavas at last reclaimed the throne of Kurujangal, their cousins, the Kauravas decided to fight them for the kingdom. They were dirty fighters, but the Pandavas remained fair to the end. Bhishma supported the Kauravas because he had sworn to defend the king. But the real heroes of the epic are the five Pandavas, specially Arjun, the archer, whose real father was Surya, the Sun.

Many years after Ganga had gone, Bhishma convinced his father to marry again. Shantanu's new queen was to be Satyavati, the daughter of a humble fisherman. But Satyavati's father was unhappy with the match.

Bhishma knew that the fisherman's real worry was that Satyavati's son could never be king, because Bhishma had first claim to the throne. But, knowing that his father had fallen in love with Satyavati, Bhishma decided to make a great sacrifice. That day when the court assembled, he summoned Satyavati and her father.

'I ask the sun, moon and stars to bear witness to my oath,' Bhishma declared. 'I will never be king of Kurujangal, nor will I father a child who can claim the throne.' He turned to Satyavati's father. 'Now do you agree to let your daughter marry my father?'

Shanatanu held up his hand. 'Take back your oath, my son, please,' he begged.

But Bhishma stood by his word.

'In that case,' said Shantanu sadly, 'may Yama let you live until you choose to die.'

And so it was that Bhishma lived to guide his nephews, the hundred Kauravas, until the Mahabharata finally reached its end.

The Rescue of Sita

This story about the kidnap and rescue of Sita is taken from the first epic, the Ramayana, which tells of the life of a great king, Rama of Ayodhya. Rama was cheated out of the throne by his evil stepmother, who insisted that Rama's father make her own son king and banish Rama and his wife Sita to the forest for fourteen years.

Rama and Sita lived happily in a cottage in the forest for many years. One day when Rama was out hunting, Sita took pity on a poor old holy man and invited him into their home. Too late Sita realised her mistake, for the old man was the demon king Ravana in disguise. He bundled Sita into his chariot and flew her back to his kingdom on the island of Lanka.

Rama searched the forest for his wife for days, but with no success. At last, in desperation, he went to the monkey king for help. The monkey general, Hanuman, was entrusted with searching Lanka to find Sita. But he could not find her anywhere.

'Show me the way, Vishnu,' Hanuman prayed, closing his eyes. When he opened them, he saw a light glowing among some trees. Hanuman leapt towards it.

'Sita!' he exclaimed. 'Rama has sent me to find you.'

Sita's hair was tangled and her clothes hung about her in tatters. She was sick with grief and despair.

'Why has it taken Rama so long to find me?' asked Sita sadly. She handed Hanuman a jewel. 'This will prove you met me. Tell Rama if he does not come soon, I will be dead.'

Hanuman's fur glowed like a flame. He was furious with Sita's captor, Ravana. He said goodbye to Sita. And as a warning to Ravana, he destroyed as much of Lanka as he could.

'How dare this monkey attack us?' Ravana thundered, releasing 80,000 warrior demons against Hanuman. But the great monkey was the son of the wind-god Vayu and as powerful as a hurricane. He leapt nimbly out of the way of the demons and their weapons.

Furious, Ravana summoned his son Indrajit. 'Kill the monkey,' he commanded. 'Use the arrow Brahma gave you. It always hits its target.' Indrajit let loose his arrow and Hanuman fell to the ground, unconscious. Ravana's demons took him to their king. Ravana's ministers wrapped Hanuman's tail in cotton wool and oil and set it alight.

'That will show Rama what we think of him,' they sneered. As Hanuman's tail burst into flames, he leapt high into the air. But he had the protection of Agni, god of fire, and felt no pain. Hanuman flew on to Ravana's fort. Lashing wildly with his tail, he smashed its towers and set its walls on fire. Then he flew directly back to Rama and told him everything. Rama's army of monkeys and bears immediately made their way down to the sea.

'Build a bridge across to Lanka,' advised Sagar, the ocean-god. Very soon Rama's troops arrived in Ravana's city. But this time the demons were ready. They knew their city better than Rama and his army and they used magic to help them. Indrajit made himself invisible and shot Rama with his special arrow. Rama collapsed, unconscious. Jambavan, king of the bears, and Hanuman were skilled healers but they could not revive Rama. Still, they did not give up hope.

As evening fell, they heard the swish of wings and felt a strong gust of air. Out of the clouds came Garuda, the eagle who belonged to Vishnu.

'I come from my master,' Garuda said. 'Vishnu fights beside those who fight on the side of right.'

Garuda enclosed Rama in his mighty wings and when he released him, Rama stood up strong and healthy.

'Take my greetings to Sita,' Rama commanded Hanuman. 'Tell her she is safe.'

Rama's troops cheered. With Vishnu's help, they knew they would win the war.

The first Indian epic, the Ramayana is read daily by many Hindus because it is said to wash away sin. According to legend, one of the Seven Sages, or Saptarishi, told a robber to repent by chanting the mantra 'ma-ra' until they returned. Seven years later, they returned to find him covered by an ant-hill, still chanting. They named him Valmiki, which means 'born from an ant-hill'. Later, Valmiki wrote down the story of the Ramayana as it unfolded before his eyes.

Death and the Healer

Yam-Raj, or Yama, is the god of death and lives with departed souls in Narg, the world of the dead. Some Hindus believe that he is the one who judges the sins of the dead and decides their punishment. When Yama goes to collect the soul from a dying body, he takes his mace and noose with him.

People are afraid of Yama because he is linked to death, but he is actually fair and kind. In one tale, he rewards a young woman who follows him past the stars and the sun to the gates of his kingdom, Narg, by returning her young husband to life. Yama is the son of Surya, the Sun.

ONCE, YAMA MARRIED A BEAUTIFUL MORTAL. Very soon, he found out that his wife had a terrible temper. When they had a son, Yama-Kumar, they battled constantly about how to bring him up.

'It's bad for the boy to see us arguing all the time,' Yama warned his wife. 'If it doesn't stop, I'll leave.' But that only started another fight, so Yama left.

Yama kept a fatherly eye on the boy as he grew. Things did not go well. Yama-Kumar grew into a lazy man with no idea of duty or prayer.

So Yama visited his son. 'If you promise to work hard, I will give you the sacred gift of healing,' he told him.

Yama-Kumar changed his ways. He worked hard, learning everything about herbs and other cures, and soon he mastered the skills of an excellent physician.

Yama was proud of the young healer and finally told him that he was his father. 'You have done well, my son,' he said. 'Here is my reward. I am always present at the sick bed. Look for me. If the patient can be healed, I will nod. But if I shake my head, the patient is incurable. You must explain that the patient is beyond help.'

'I will do as you say,' Yama-Kumar replied.

Yama-Kumar soon gained fame as an excellent physician, so when the king's daughter grew ill, he was naturally the one to be summoned to her bedside.

As usual, Yama-Kumar looked for his father. And there Yama stood, swinging his noose with one hand while he held his mace in the other. Grimly, he shook his head.

'Please let her live, Father,' Yama-Kumar begged.

'She is too young and well-loved to die.'

Yama did not like being challenged. But his son had never argued with him before, so he gave in. 'You have three days,' he hissed.

The healer thanked his father and began to tend the princess. He worked tirelessly and soon she was better. But Yama-Kumar knew this did not matter if Yama did not change his mind. As promised, Yama arrived on the third day. The healer looked up casually from his patient's bedside. 'Oh father,' he said, 'mother's been asking about you. Perhaps you'd be good enough to see her?'

Yama turned pale. 'Never!' he shuddered. 'Please, don't tell her where I am, or she'll follow me back to the land of the dead.'

Yama-Kumar laughed softly to himself. 'We can make a deal,' he offered. 'Leave the princess here and I promise to keep my mother away from you.'

When Yama had recovered from the shock, he chuckled. 'I like a man with wit. You can save your patient. She will live to be a very old lady.'

And so saying, he went about his business.

Trishankhu and the Sages

The Seven Sages (Saptarishi) were men of power and magic who often outdid the gods. But even they could not overturn the rules of heaven. The two sages in this story were deadly rivals. According to some Hindu writings, the Saptarishi still shine in the night sky in the constellation called the Ursa Major.

Surabhi emerged when the gods churned the Ocean of Milk. She had magical powers, and once helped the sage Vasishta by producing a troop of warriors to fight an evil king. Surabhi was also said to be able to grant all desires. It is probably because of her that cows are sacred to Hindus.

KING TRISHANKHU WANTED TO GO TO SVARG, THE HEAVEN OF THE GODS.

'If you atone for your sins, your soul will go there,' Vasishta, chief sage of the Saptarishi, told him.

Many years before, when Trishankhu was a young prince, he had abducted a woman from her home. His father had banished him from his kingdom for twelve years, saying, 'You can't simply take what you want.'

Trishankhu returned the woman to her home. While in exile in the forest, he tried hard to make amends. Every day he left food for the family of Vishvamitra, an old sage who was away on a mission. Then famine came. There were no animals to hunt and no berries or nuts to pick. The prince was so hungry that he killed Vasishta's cow, Surabhi, and ate her. Vasishta was grief-stricken.

'You will be known as Trishankhu from now on,' he cursed. 'He of the three sins. You abducted a woman, you killed a cow and you ate her flesh.'

When the twelve years of exile were over, Trishankhu returned to his kingdom. Soon, he inherited the throne.

'I will do my duty and advise the new king fairly,' the sage Vasishta decided. 'But I will never truly respect him.'

And now Trishankhu was once again showing the side of his character that Vasishta disliked.

'But I want to go to Svarg now,' Trishankhu sulked.

'Perform a ceremony. Make a sacrifice. Just get me to the heaven of the gods!'

Vasishta refused. This man could not simply demand what he wanted. 'I will not insult the gods by breaking their laws.'

'Well then,' Trishankhu said, 'I'll ask Vishvamitra instead.'

Vishvamitra remembered Trishankhu's kindness to his family during his long years of exile. 'I'll do my best,' he promised. Vishvamitra lit a sacrificial fire and fed it many rich offerings. He chanted holy words, making the flames prance higher and higher. Suddenly, he pushed Trishankhu upwards. The king rose up on the flames, floating towards heaven.

But Indra, king of Svarg, held up a hand and Trishankhu hurtled back. Vishvamitra waved him up, and for a while Trishankhu tumbled back and forth between heaven and Earth.

'Stop!' bellowed Vishvamitra, suspending Trishankhu mid-heaven. 'Or I will create a new heaven for this man.'

Indra knew the old sage's power. He thought quickly. 'Can we leave Trishankhu where he is?'

Vishvamitra agreed and created a new constellation around the king. And to this day, Trishankhu shines brightly in the night sky.

TALES FROM AFRICAN MYTHS

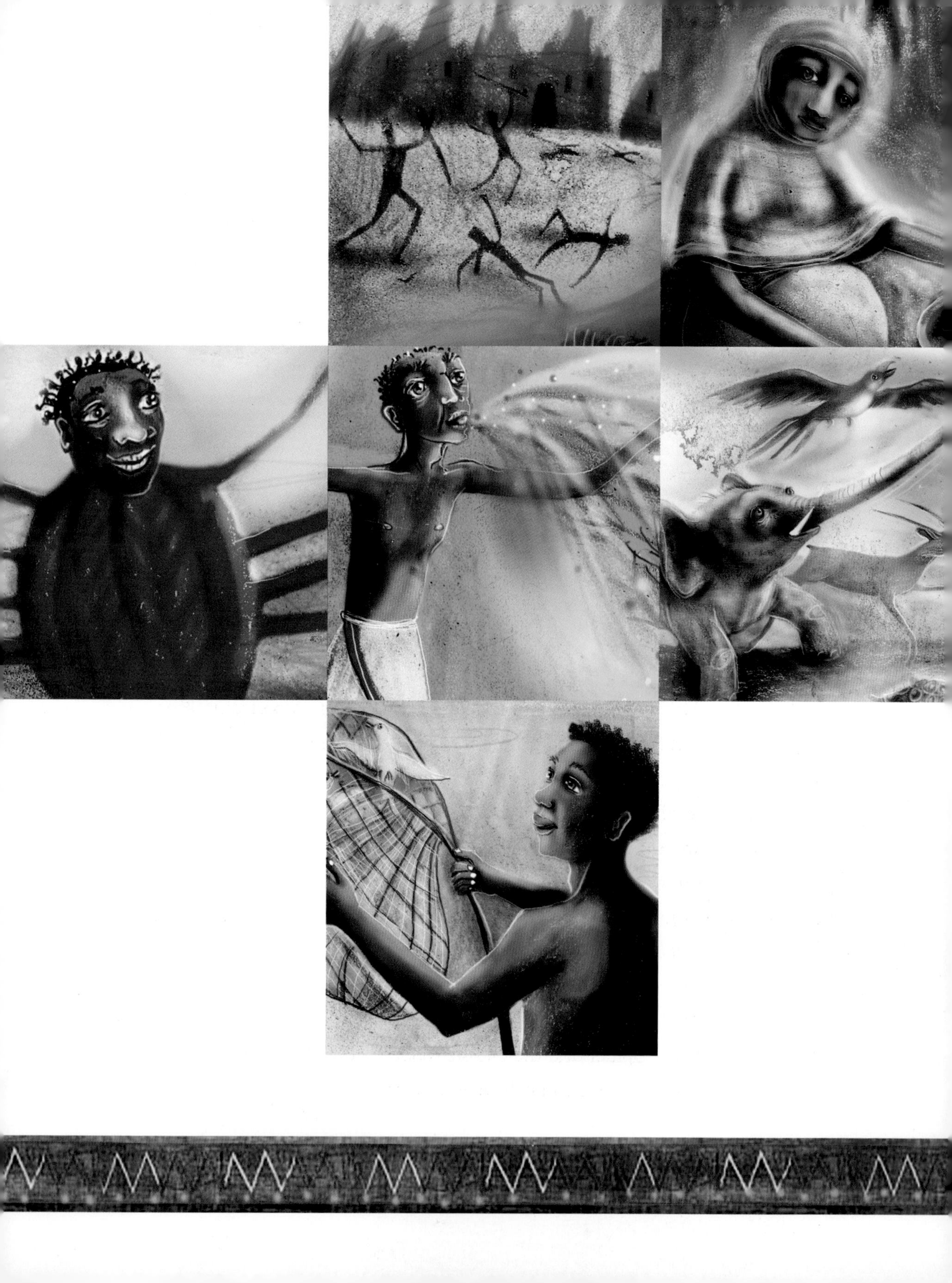

INTRODUCTION

Africa is a large continent with many different countries with dozens of their own tribes, each with their own storytelling tradition. Elements common to most of the stories are respect for wild creatures, the dangers and gifts of the bush or wilderness, and the importance of nature. Drought, which is a serious threat to the lives of people living off the land in a hot country, is also a common feature. Spiders regularly appear in African myths – perhaps because of their mysterious ability to weave webs and create a link between heaven and Earth. Probably the most famous character of African myths is the loveable Anansi, a spider-god.

The myths of Africa survive through being remembered and told within families and clans, and also because the gods and goddesses are still part of African worship. Many stories have been lost and some survive only in fragments, though, thankfully, in the last couple of centuries, people have begun to write them down. Myths about many African gods and goddesses, such as Shango and Oya, have travelled out of Africa to other parts of the world like South America and the Caribbean, where the characters have been transformed into local saints.

African myths are similar to others in their focus on birth, death and the afterlife. In the first story we learn how Yorubaland, believed by the Yoruba tribe to be the centre of the world, was created by Oduduwa, son of the supreme god Olodumare. In another, we learn how Man and Woman came to live on Earth and upset all the animals, as well as the creator god Mulunge, with their lack of respect for their natural environment (pages 148-149). The story of Kitamba's wife (pages 164-165) illustrates the ancient African belief in the underworld, while the Spider and the Ghosts (pages 150-151) describes the ghosts that some Africans still believe lurk in the wilderness.

How Yorubaland was Created

The Yoruba people of Nigeria, West Africa, believed that Olodumare, god of the heavens, sent his children down to create the world. They created Ife, which became the centre of Yorubaland and the world. This creation myth teaches the moral that it pays to be active and make the best of what you have.

OLODUMARE, GREAT GOD OF THE HEAVENS, DECIDED IT WAS TIME HIS SONS OBATALA AND ODUDUWA DID SOMETHING USEFUL.

'Step down into the world,' he commanded his sons. 'Here are three gifts that will help you.'

The two young men took the three bags. They peered down. For miles and miles, all they could see was swirling water. So Olodumare created a palm tree and gave his sons a gentle push. They landed safely among the large fronds of the palm.

Obatala, the older brother, fumbled around among the branches. He cut a small hole in the trunk of the tree. Immediately, frothy liquid gushed out. It was sweet and it made Obatala feel good. He drank his fill of the palm wine, then fell asleep.

His brother Oduduwa was very different. He climbed down the trunk of the palm and stood in the cool water. Then he opened the first bag from his father and started to empty out some of its contents. White sand flowed onto the surface of the waters. Oduduwa opened the second bag. A chameleon scurried out. Carefully, slowly, one by one, it placed its feet on the sand. Oduduwa watched it with interest.

'This ground is firm,' he thought. 'I can walk on it.'

Oduduwa emptied out the remains of the second bag – it was black soil. Then he opened the third bag. Out came a chicken and began scratching around for food. Sand and soil flew in all directions, forming solid pieces of land on the water as far as the eye could see. This land came to be called Ife.

Olodumare looked down happily. His son had done well. So he sent Aje, goddess of wealth, down to Ife.

'Your father has sent you more gifts,' Aje told Oduduwa. 'Iron bars to make weapons, tools to prepare the Earth and maize seeds to grow crops in it.'

And that was how farming began and people could live on Earth.

When the world was created, Olodumare appointed the chief gods and they created the different Yoruba clans. The Yoruba people split into many more clans as time went on, and the gods in this story were given different names. In some myths, Oduduwa is described as a goddess who was sent down to Earth after her brother, Obatala, failed to achieve anything. Aje came along to help her.

Dzivaguru's Curse

Long ago, Dzivaguru was the mother goddess of the Shona-speaking people of Korekore in Zimbabwe. Her story answers fundamental questions about nature, such as why we have day and night, rain and drought.

DZIVAGURU LIVED IN A BEAUTIFUL PALACE BY A LAKE. HER VALLEY WAS LUSH AND FILLED WITH CATTLE, GOATS AND SHEEP. Her people loved her because she was kind. She brought rain to nourish the land, sunshine to warm the people and the darkness of night for them to rest.

Nosenga, son of the sky-god, looked down at Dzivaguru's wealth and her power. He was jealous.

'I will go down to Earth,' he decided, 'and take Dzivaguru's rich kingdom for myself.'

But Dzivaguru knew what was in Nosenga's mind. She would not give up her lands without a fight. 'Fog!' she commanded, 'fill the valley. Light! Follow me.'

Then she climbed to the top of a mountain and watched. When Nosenga arrived in her land, he was surrounded by darkness. All he could see was the shape of the distant hills and the dim glow of the sky. But that was no good. He wanted the goddess's palace and her livestock and her wonderful, glittering lake.

Nosenga knew that Dzivaguru, goddess of dark and light, owned two golden Sunbirds. To bring sunshine, she lured the birds to her and trapped the sun for while. 'I won't let her beat me,' Nosenga vowed. 'I will trap her Sunbirds.'

So Nosenga created a magical trap and soon snared both the Sunbirds. Instantly the sun began to glow in the distance and dawn broke.

Over the hills, Dzivaguru appeared. 'Nosenga!' she declared. 'I will punish you for snatching away my land. People will only worship you for a short time. You, too, will be replaced by outsiders. Because you trapped my Sunbirds and brought out the sun, the land will heat up and become parched. For every sin your sons commit, I will hold back the rain and drought will follow.'

And with those words, Dzivaguru disappeared forever. But people remembered her words whenever there was drought or their land was invaded.

Two images of a pair of golden birds which look like swallows were found in a ruined temple in Zimbabwe about a hundred years ago. They are probably the Sunbirds mentioned in the myth of Dzivaguru. Stories in the Shona language often praise swallows for their swiftness. They migrate to Zimbabwe in spring, appearing when the sun grows stronger after winter, so they are closely connected with the sun as this myth shows.

Oya Steals Magic from Shango

Shango, the Earth god, was created at the beginning of the world when Olodumare and his sons made Yorubaland. He was immensely powerful, but he wanted even greater might. After a long time ruling the Kingdom of Oyo on Earth, he travelled up to the skies on a long golden chain.

SHANGO'S THIRD WIFE, OYA, STOOD BEFORE ESHU, THE SHAMAN.

'My husband has sent me to fetch the medicine you made for him,' she said, offering him a goat in exchange. Eshu handed Oya a small package.

'How is it to be used?' Oya asked.

Eshu smiled. 'Let Shango work it out.'

Oya thanked Eshu and went on her way. But she was extremely curious.

'It won't do any harm to look,' she thought, unwrapping the package.

Inside was a glowing, red powder. Oya dipped her finger into it.

'Shango won't notice if I taste a tiny bit.' She popped her finger in her mouth. It was tasteless. Disappointed, Oya wrapped up the parcel and went home.

'How shall I use it?' Shango asked when Oya gave him the medicine.

Oya opened her mouth to reply, but out shot a bright tongue of fire. Eshu's magic was working!

'You stole my magic!' Shango thundered.

Terrified, Oya ran and hid among a flock of sheep. But Shango was close behind and hurled thunderstones at the sheep who had huddled around her. One by one, they fell dead and Oya hid herself among their bodies.

Shango stormed off to a nearby hill to see if there was any magic left. He opened the package. Most of the red powder was still there. He put some on his lips and took a deep breath. A tongue of fire leapt from his mouth, the same as Oya's.

But he wanted to be more powerful. He took a second taste. The fire shot out further. And a third. The flames burst from his nose. Shango consumed all the magic. He breathed in, letting the air fill his lungs. Then he exhaled. Arms of fire came from his mouth and nose, catching the trees around him. They spread to the buildings until Shango's city was in flames. People ran everywhere as their homes burnt down before their eyes.

Shango's people soon built a new city but people always remembered how the furious breath of Shango, Lord of Thunder, could burn down a whole city. To this day, when lightning strikes, they call 'Kabiyesi!' which means 'Greetings, your majesty.'

Oya is the goddess of the river Niger in west Africa. She was the youngest of Shango's three wives and his favourite. She is sometimes depicted as a goddess with eight heads, each representing a tributary or branch of the river.

Mulunge Escapes the Humans

The spider appears in many African myths, perhaps because of its ability to weave webs and spin a thread that links heaven and Earth, as in this story. This myth from Lake Malawi tells us about the beliefs of the Yao people. They hunted to survive, but showed deep respect for their natural environment and the creatures who shared it with them.

CHAMELEON WAS VERY HUNGRY. 'I wonder what I've caught today,' he thought, pulling in his trap from the river. There were two very strange creatures inside. He took the trap to Mulunge, the Creator, who had made him and all the other creatures living peacefully together in the world.

'They are humans: a Man and a Woman,' Mulunge told him. 'Release them from the trap and watch.'

Man and Woman grew tall and strong. They took bits of wood and rubbed them together until sparks flew and they burst into flames. Man and Woman killed a buffalo, roasted it on the fire and ate it. From that day on, they cut down trees, lit fires and killed animals each day.

Mulunge the Creator was very upset. Man and Woman were destroying his world.

'Who will they kill next?' whispered the animals. 'Who will be scorched to death on their fires?'

The creatures of the jungle became scared and took refuge all over the world. Mulunge was not afraid of the humans, but he was sad and lonely. And he no longer enjoyed living in his world.

One day, Mulunge saw Spider up in the sky.

'How did you get there, my friend?' he called out.

Spider spun him a thread and Mulunge latched on to it and climbed until he too was in the sky. And that is where he stayed because the cruelty and carelessness of humans had driven him away from the world.

The Ngombe of the Congo region tell a similar tale about their creator god escaping into the jungle from quarrelsome people. As a result, we cannot see god and do not know what he looks like. In the Barotse version from Upper Zambezi, the escaped god Nyambi becomes the sun and his wife Nasilele, the moon. In all these stories, it is the selfish behaviour of humans that causes conflict and unhappiness.

The Spider and the Ghosts

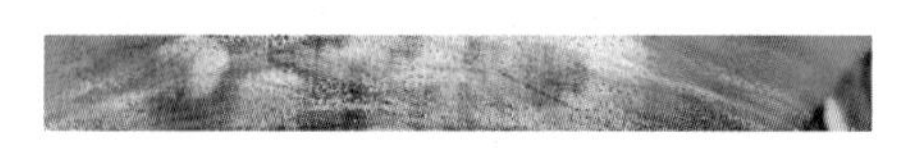

Most African traditions tell us that after death, a part of us called the spirit or soul, continues to live. This may be in the most unreachable parts of a forest, beneath river beds or in the darkest caves or tunnels. The souls that live longest are those of strong people such as chiefs, mothers and much-loved people. They are happy and they stay around their families to help them.

A MAN AND HIS WIFE WERE CROSSING A RIVER WHEN THEY HEARD A VOICE. It was asking to be carried across the river. The man looked down and saw that the request had come from a skull.

'No!' said the man. 'How do I know that you won't hurt me?'

'Please help it,' said his wife. 'It can't harm us.'

When they had crossed the river, the man bent to put the skull down. But it clamped his hand in its teeth and would not let go. The skull forced the man to put it on his shoulder and walk on until they came to the bush.

'Go that way,' the skull commanded.

'It looks dangerous in there,' the man pleaded.

'Do as I say,' hissed the skull and bit the man's neck hard. The man cried out in pain and obeyed.

Finally they came to a clearing with a few shacks falling to pieces and covered in undergrowth. Something brushed against the woman's face. She screamed and scratched at her hair. Something had become entangled in it. The next moment the air was thick with the spirits of the dead, flitting about, cheering the skull.

'Meat,' they hissed. 'Good food to fill our bellies.'

'Fetch some wood,' snarled the skull. 'And don't try to run away because we can track you down by your smell, wherever you go.'

'It's a fine thing you're asking us to do,' snapped the man. 'Why should we help you make the fire to cook us alive?'

The spirits swarmed around the couple till they could hardly breathe.

'Now, will you fetch the wood?' the skull demanded.

Quietly, the man and woman went to collect firewood. After a while, the woman sat down, weeping to herself. She grasped half-heartedly at the pile of dead twigs lying beside her. Out crawled a small spider.

'Why are you crying?' asked the spider.

'We're collecting wood,' replied the woman, 'so that the ghosts can light a fire to cook us on.'

'I'll help you,' said the spider. 'But you must promise not to disturb my home again.'

'Gladly,' replied the man and woman together.

Immediately, the spider set to work. It spun a huge web around the clearing where the ghosts were huddled. Round and round it went, until the entire space was wrapped up in a massive web. The ghosts thrashed against it but the web held firm. They were trapped.

The man and his wife thanked the spider whole-heartedly. 'You saved our lives,' they said. 'We promise that neither we, nor our descendants, will ever again harm a spider.'

Tales from all over Africa describe ghosts as skeletons of the dead who give the illusion of having white, human bodies. They love meat, especially the flesh of humans, because they hope that it will put flesh on their own bones. They can speak to people, and, as in this story, only appear in wild, deserted places in the deep of night.

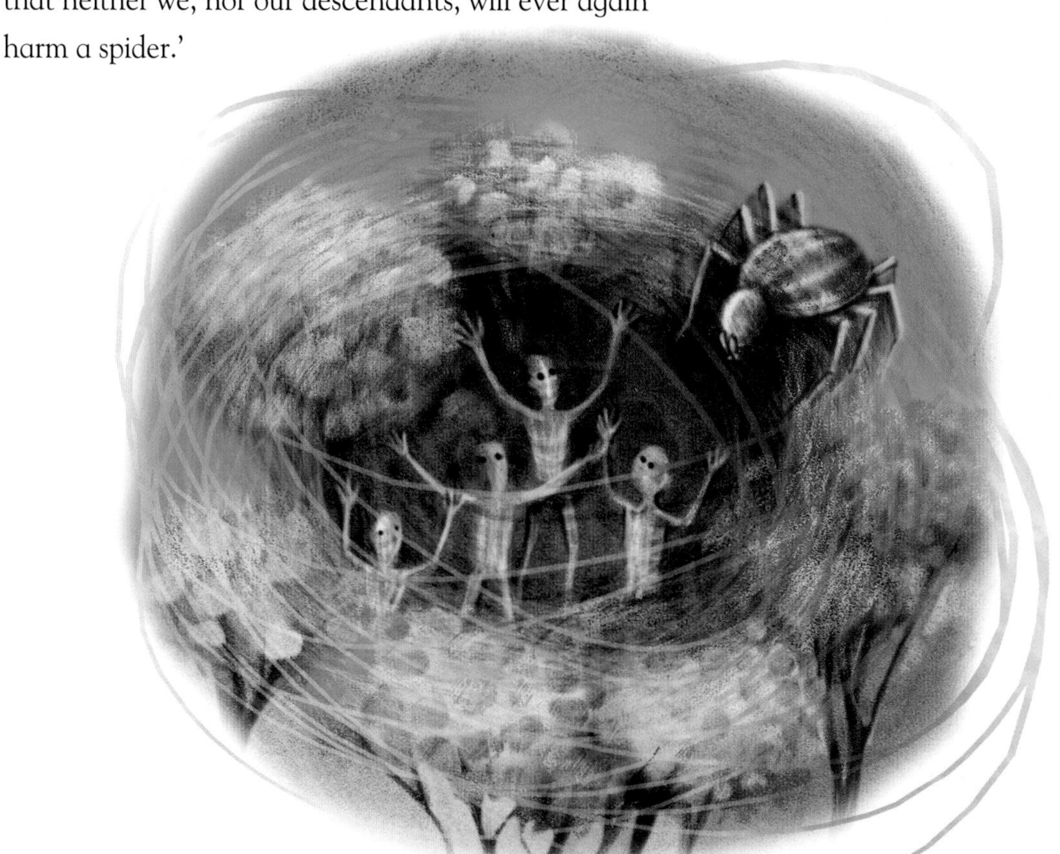

Anansi and the stories

The Spider-god Anansi is a trickster, or a culture hero – a character much loved and admired for his cleverness and his ability to get the better of others. His stories began in Ghana, West Africa, but have travelled across the world to the West Indies and parts of America.

ANANSI LOVED STORIES. Everywhere he looked there were stories, terrible ones and wonderful ones, funny ones and sad ones. They made people laugh and cry and taught them to be brave and helpful and good. There was only one thing that annoyed him about stories – they belonged to someone else. So Anansi made up his mind to own all the stories in the world.

'Sell me the stories,' he said to Onyame, the Supreme God, who created everything on heaven and Earth. 'I will pay any price.'

'Many people have asked,' Onyame laughed. 'But no one has brought me what I want yet.'

'Then they did not want the stories as much as I do,' insisted Anansi, who could never resist a challenge.

'Bring me the bees, the python and the leopard,' Onyame said. 'And you will be Lord of Stories.'

'I'm on my way,' said Anansi, setting off. He did not stop until he came to a stream. He collected a jar of water and an empty gourd with a hole in it. He knew exactly where to find some bees and when he got there, he hurled the water at their hive. The bees scattered, buzzing loudly.

'It's raining,' yelled Anansi, holding up his gourd. 'Fly into this and you'll keep dry.'

The bees flew into the gourd and Anansi stuffed the hole up with grass. He had captured the bees. His first task was complete.

Now Anansi walked deep into the jungle where the river flowed. 'Ho, Lord Python!' he called. 'I need you to settle an argument.'

Python crawled out from the river's edge. 'Why are you shouting?' he grumbled.

'See this?' Anansi said, holding out a pole. 'My wife insists you're shorter and weedier than this. I told her you are longer and sturdier.'

Onyame was the supreme god of the Ashanti of West Africa. His name meant sky, but he was often worshipped in the form of a tree-trunk. He was the creator-god, who brought rain to the people and helped those in need. He has many other names, including Nzambi and Nyame.

Python shuffled forward, squinting at the pole. 'I will lie beside it,' he hissed. 'Then you can measure me up and prove who is right.'

Anansi shook his head. 'My wife's a stubborn woman. She'll have to see it for herself.'

So Python lay down beside the pole and Anansi bound him to it. That was the second job done.

Finally, it was time to snare the leopard. Anansi knew where Leopard hunted, so he made his way to the spot and dug a deep ditch in his path which he covered with brush, mud and grass. Then he found a quiet hiding place and went to sleep. Very soon, he was woken by a loud roar.

'Get me out of here!'

Anansi went over to the ditch. 'I would help,' he called down to Leopard. 'But you are vicious by nature. You'll eat me the moment you're safe.'

'I won't,' promised Leopard. 'Help me or I'll starve to death down here.'

Anansi pushed down the sturdy branch of a tree which was growing beside the ditch.

'Tie your hind legs to this,' he called out, lowering a rope to Leopard. 'I will hold it down.'

Leopard did as Anansi asked.

'Get ready,' called Anansi. Then suddenly, without warning, he let go. The branch sprung back with Leopard hanging upside down. He struggled and kicked, shouting, 'Anansi, cut me down!'

'At once,' replied Anansi, chuckling. He held out a sack and cut the rope. Leopard fell into it. Immediately, Anansi fastened the mouth of the sack with the rope.

Anansi's mission was complete. He took all his trophies to Onyame.

'You have proved that with determination and a little wit, you can achieve anything,' Onyame said, very pleased that someone had at last brought him the creatures he had wanted for so long.

And from that day on, all stories belonged to Anansi.

Miseke and the Thunder God

This story comes from Rwanda, where the Thunder-god was considered Lord of the Heavens. The elements of nature such as rain, thunder and storms were an important part of the lives of ancient people. They made offerings to the elements in return for their favours.

KWISABA HAD GONE TO WAR AND HIS WIFE WAS TIRED AND HUNGRY. There was no one to share the household tasks while she awaited her baby's birth. A storm was coming and though she tried and tried, she could not light a fire to cook with. She looked up at the sky in despair.

'Someone, please light this fire for me,' she prayed, 'even if it is Thunder himself.'

Lightning cracked and thunder boomed, and the next moment a tall man appeared beside her.

'I'll answer your prayer,' said the man. 'But in return I want your first-born if she is a daughter.'

The woman agreed and the man, who was Thunder, lit her fire, chopped up a great pile of wood and left.

Soon, the war ended. Kwisaba returned home to find his wife living in comfort with a new daughter, Miseke.

'You are indeed a daughter to be proud of,' Kwisaba laughed, as he played with his baby girl. 'One day, we will find you a handsome husband and get a fine bride price.'

'It's time to tell him my promise to Thunder,' thought Kwisaba's wife.

'We will keep Miseke safe inside the house,' Kwisaba decided, when his wife had confessed. 'Thunder can't take her when she's inside.'

So Miseke stayed inside the house, except in fair weather when there was no sign of thunder and her parents let her play with her friends in the yard.

Miseke grew older and more beautiful and, one day, her friends noticed beads and

When a couple were to be married, it was the tradition for the groom's side of the family to pay the bride-price. This was usually cattle, or some valuable grain or nuts, though in modern times it is often cash. The families met to agree the price, which was meant to be a token of respect and friendship between the two families.

bangles fall from her mouth as she spoke.

'Thunder is giving Miseke gifts, just as you did when you were wooing me,' her mother said to Kwisaba.

'It is time to lock her up,' Kwisaba decided.

From that day on Miseke was forbidden to go out with the other girls. But one day, Kwisaba and his wife were called away on a long trip and Miseke slipped out and went to the river with her friends. Happily, they played, sang and danced until a dark cloud appeared in the sky. It rolled towards them, then dipped. There was a deep rumble, followed by lightning. The cloud scooped up Miseke in its folds, and floated swiftly up to the skies. Thunder had taken his wife. Miseke's parents were heartbroken.

'How will he treat her?' they wept. But they need not have worried. Miseke lived happily for many years with her husband and children, in a wonderful palace filled with everything she wanted. But often she thought of her parents and then she would become a little sad.

'Go to visit them,' Thunder said one day, kindly. 'But keep to the paths.'

Overjoyed, Miseke made her way down to Earth, accompanied by her children, cattle, pots of beer and servants to help her. Soon they arrived in the forest near her village. As they got closer, the path vanished. They were lost.

'Give me food!' a voice boomed. Before her, Miseke saw a massive ogre.

'Give him the cattle!' Miseke ordered her servants.

But that was not enough. In no time at all, the ogre had eaten the cattle, drunk

the beer and swallowed the servants. Swiftly, Miseke told her eldest son to look for the river and follow its course to the village for help. She clung to the children who remained with her, praying that help would come. But by morning the ogre was hungry again and began demanding Miseke's children.

Just in time came the sound of loud drum beats. Miseke saw fire brands blazing in the distance. The next moment, her father appeared out of the brush, followed by her son and other villagers.

'Miseke,' they called. 'You are home at last!'

Together, the men killed the ogre. The village shaman cut off the ogre's big toe and all Miseke's possessions suddenly re-appeared before her.

Monsters and ogres are found in myths from all over Africa. Most often these are giants. One particular kind of monster is portrayed as a huge mouth which shouts the word hungry, as it runs about looking for victims. People who see it are too terrified to run and the monster gobbles them up easily.

Miseke's parents prepared a great wedding feast and asked Miseke and her children all about their life in the skies. But soon it was time to return. The villagers gave Miseke many presents and gathered outside to say goodbye.

Suddenly, the skies grew dark. Lightning flashed, thunder rumbled and a great purple cloud scooped up Miseke and her children, along with all the gifts. That was the last Kwisaba and his wife saw of Miseke. But they knew she lived in comfort and bliss and that made them happy.

Ghasir's Lute

This story comes from the Epic of Dausi, which the anthropologist Leo Frobenius wrote between 1899 and 1915. The Epic consists of a group of songs about the mythical African city of Wagadu in West Africa, which was destroyed and rebuilt many times. The story of Ghasir and his lute is the first part. An epic is a grand tale of heroes, often told in poetry.

PRINCE GHASIR RODE BACK FROM THE BATTLE. The Borduma tribe wanted to conquer the great kingdom of Wagadu and as long as their soldiers kept attacking, Ghasir's men would fight.

'Oho Ghasir!' a voice hailed him. 'Why do you go to war? You will never be king of Wagadu.'

Ghasir was angry. 'Show yourself!' he commanded.

An old man stepped out of the shadows.

'Kiekorri,' Ghasir said, recognising the sage. 'What do you mean I'll never be king?'

'I mean what I say. You may be a brave warrior and a hero, but you will never wear your father's crown.'

'You're wrong!' declared Ghasir, drawing his sword.

'Killing me will not change your fate, Ghasir,' Kiekorri laughed. 'It is better to go into the forest where the wild birds sing. They'll tell you what's in store for you.'

Ghasir spurred his horse towards the woodland where the birds flocked. 'How will I know what they say?' he wondered, as he dismounted from his horse.

As he walked towards the bushes, a large woodcock appeared in the clearing. It threw back its head and began to sing.

'I can understand its words,' Ghasir realised, amazed. The bird was singing about a story. It said that it would be a mighty story, told in a song that would last forever, far beyond heroic deeds and mighty warriors because its words held the power of truth and heartbreak and love.

Ghasir was enchanted by the song. 'Kiekorri,' he reported back to the sage. 'I heard the woodcock and understood his words.'

'So that is your fate!' said Kieokorri. 'Your destiny is to be a poet, not a fighter. What are you waiting for? Don't all good poets have lutes?'

Ghasir sought out the best lutemaker in all of Wagadu and when his lute was ready, he tried its strings. But the lute was silent.

'What's this?' he thundered at the lutemaker.

'I am just a craftsman,' the lutemaker replied, shaking with fear because he knew that those who displeased Ghasir were likely to have their hearts impaled on a sharp weapon. 'I can only craft the instrument. And this is the best I've ever made. But only creatures that bleed and breathe have a voice. Your lute will sing if you take it to battle with you. Attach it to your shoulder, let it become part of you.

The Epic tells us that Ghasir belonged to the Fasa dynasty. This may be one of the reasons that African scholar Dr. Jan Knappert writes that the mythical city of Wagadu may be the present capital of Burkina Faso, also spelled Ougadougu. In the full version of the story, the wanderings of Ghasir and his family through northern Libya, south to Niger, Benin and Burkina Faso, may show the migration of tribes long ago.

Let your blood run through it and let it breathe your breath. Only then will it sing the song you want to hear.'

Ghasir summoned his sons. 'There is nothing greater than reputation,' he said. 'You and I, we fight every day. Our deeds end with the battle. But words live beyond us. If we want our deeds remembered, we must fight even harder to be part of a great song that will live forever.'

For seven days Ghasir fought harder than ever before. So did his sons, urged on by the desire for fame. Each night Ghasir arrived home, full of sorrow, with a dead son over his shoulder. And his tears of grief mingled with the blood of his dead sons and drenched the silent lute. But the Borduma kept coming.

On the eighth day of battle, the people of Wagadu came to Ghasir. 'Please end this bloody war,' they pleaded. 'We long for peace. You have already sacrificed seven sons for the sake of fame. Take what is left of your family and leave us in peace.'

Ghasir accepted the wishes of his people and went into the bush. There, near the desert, he spent many years herding cattle.

One night, when his companions were asleep, he sat beneath the dark Sahara sky, watching the huge patterns formed by the stars. He thought of his dead sons and his father who had passed away, leaving Wagadu without a ruler. He remembered stories of how the Borduma came after he had left and his people opened the gates of Wagadu, saying they wanted peace. Yet the Borduma ravaged the crops, pillaged the granaries and razed the houses to the ground, leaving behind only rubble and dust. Ghasir's heart filled with sadness. And then he heard a song. It was speaking his thoughts. Who was singing it?

Ghasir held out his precious lute and listened to the verses pouring from it. And tears streamed from the eyes of the warrior that had been held in since he was a child.

'It is true, after all,' he wept. 'This is the song that will last forever.'

And so it is that the Epic of Dausi is told to this day.

Kitamba's Wife

This story from the Mbundu people of Angola shows their belief that the dead cross over to continue life in another world, often in the same form. Their god of death, Kalunga-Ngombe, lives underground, unlike other gods. Kalunga says in another story that he kills for a reason and that he is not cruel. But once someone has seen him death usually follows.

QUEEN MULONGO HAD DIED AND HER HUSBAND, KING KITAMBA, WAS SO UNHAPPY THAT HE MADE THE WHOLE VILLAGE MOURN WITH HIM. Ordinary life had come to a standstill. So the people sent a village elder to get the advice of the kimbanda, a wise man with powerful medicine.

'The queen is dead, but we must carry on with our lives,' said the elder. 'What shall we do?

The kimbanda thought a moment, then replied,

'I will go and find the queen in the kingdom of Kalunga to get her advice.'

When the elder had left, the kimbanda dug a deep hole in the ground of his hut, directly in front of his fireplace. 'I'm going down this hole,' he told his wife. 'Water it well each day I'm away so that the soils stays soft and loose. Do not stop thinking of me and keep praying for my return.'

The kimbanda descended into the hole and found himself on a long road, which he followed until he came to a small group of people. Among them was Queen Mulongo, peacefully weaving a basket. The kimbanda greeted the queen politely.

'Your husband mourns you day and night,' he said. 'Can you return to the world of the living to comfort him?'

Mulongo looked up from her weaving. 'Do you see that man on the big chair?' she asked, pointing. 'He is Kalunga-Ngombe, the Lord of Death. Once he takes someone away, they can never return to the world of the living. But I am happy here.'

Mulongo leaned forward and whispered a message to the kimbanda. Then she took a band from her arm and gave it to him. 'This will prove to Kitamba that you have spoken to me. Eat nothing while you are in Kalunga's kingdom or you will have to remain here.'

The kimbanda thanked the queen politely and returned to his home through the hole in the ground. He thanked his wife and set off immediately to see Kitamba.

'Queen Mulongo has sent you a message,' he said, showing him the arm-band for proof. 'Stop your mourning because you will meet her very soon.'

Kitamba was happy again. 'Let my people resume their lives,' he proclaimed. 'Let them pound their grain and fetch water from the river. Let their children sing and play. Mulongo and I will soon be together again.'

The kimbanda in this story is a kind of shaman - a holy man, who is in touch with the spirits and has the power of healing. In times of need, his people seek his help and he is able to travel to other worlds in order to ask for the help of the gods or the dead. Sometimes this involves a burial ceremony like the one described in this story.

INDEX